To Italy, with Love

and other stories

by

Fiona Zedde

Also by the Author

<u>Novels</u>

Bliss
A Taste of Sin
Every Dark Desire
Desire at Dawn
Hungry for It
Dangerous Pleasures
Broken in Soft Places

<u>Available July 2016</u>

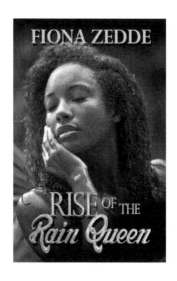

Acknowledgments

Although this collection is not what I set out to write when I packed my bags and headed to Europe in 2014, this is one of the completed projects that came out of that trip. The other story, a historical novel set in France in the 1920's, is still growing and changing from its home on my hard drive, becoming both more complex and long range than I imagined.

Even though that story is still in its chrysalis, I want to thank everyone who made that research trip possible and supported me through the process. I can't say enough how much your help meant to me. Thank you Anna Stevens, Benita Parker Myers, Bashante Rogers, Sheree L Greer, Juanita Davis, Andres Melendez-Salgado, Roland Royster, DeAnna Scott, Zakiya Johnson Lord, and everyone else who helped to make the research trip a reality.

Thank you so very much to Angela Gabriel for helping with the tweaks, plot turns, and dangling whatevers. You're the best. And to Jay Odon, my first official beta reader, Thank You for providing the last minute eyes!

And, always and forever, THANK YOU to my readers. You make this whole crazy journey worth it.

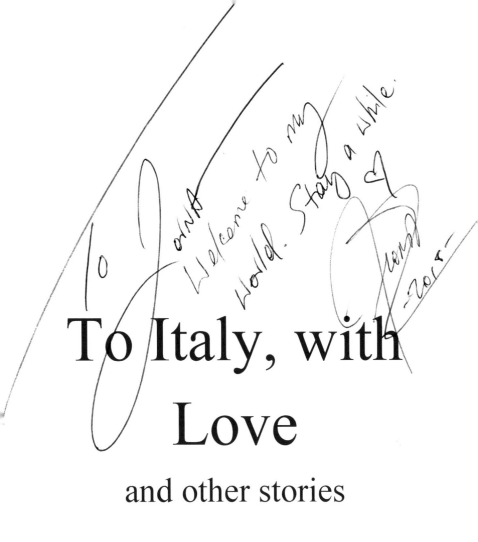

To Jamie
Welcome to my
World. Stay a while. ♡

— 2015 —

To Italy, with Love

Love

and other stories

"To Italy with Love"

Chapter 1

"So are you going to stop being bisexual now that you're suddenly marrying a guy?"

Silence, heavy and thick, dropped over the sunny Italian terrace where seven women lay, half-dozing in a post-dinner haze. Iris stared at the one who'd spoken, Chrisanne, in disbelief. Aisha, the bride-to-be, only shook her head, smiling at the much younger girl in amusement. She didn't look at all insulted.

"I wouldn't say sudden," Aisha said. She rolled over on the lounge chair and closed her eyes as if that was all that needed to be said.

Iris sat up in her chair, cradling her glass of limoncello against a spill, and came to her friend's defense, although Aisha was usually the last person who needed defending. "I doubt it's sudden since she's marrying the guy she's been openly dating for two years." She wrinkled her nose like she smelled something bad.

Chrisanne was a stranger to Iris. They'd met less than a day before when Chrisanne arrived at the villa where Aisha was already hosting the bridal party in preparation for her wedding. Iris didn't even know how Aisha met Chrisanne, a Jamaican-born girl in her mid twenties who'd just graduated from college and was rude as hell. Iris was Jamaican too but felt no solidarity with the girl. What was

1

Chrisanne thinking challenging Aisha like that? That wasn't the kind of thing you said to anybody on the weekend of their wedding.

"It's cool, Iris." Aisha made a dismissive motion with her own glass of limoncello, dripping some of the liqueur over the back of her hand. "That's just how she is. It's okay."

Chrisanne, who'd coincidentally been in Italy for the summer as a present to herself before starting a new job at some big accounting firm, had basically invited herself to the wedding. Aisha was too much of a sweetheart to say no to the loudmouthed girl. All four bridesmaids looked at her like they wanted to strangle her, including Iris, who was the maid of honor and never before thought of herself as a violent person.

"Bitch, chill." Imani, one of the bridesmaids, said. She was from Philly, had been one of the first straight women to accept and love Aisha after she left the land of the pussy eaters. She would also undeniably be the first to slap a bitch—that bitch being Chrisanne—if she stepped out of line.

But Chrisanne apparently wasn't one to take a subtle hint to shut the hell up. "What? I'm just curious." She waved around her martini glass from the wide stone railing of the balcony where she sat, precariously balanced. A girl who liked to literally be on the edge. Far below her, the sea lapped at the cliff-strewn coast line. The pink liquid sloshed around in her martini glass but did not spill. "I'd never heard of something like this in my life. In my world, you're either a dyke or a bi-curious chick out to get your rocks off having some girl eat your pussy for a few months. I've never known of a die-hard lezzie all of a sudden deciding she didn't like the taste of pussy anymore and going so far as to latch on full time, marriage and all, to the dick."

Iris was starting to seriously re-think her stance on violence. "If you think Aisha is some sort of traitor to lesbians by living her own damn life then you better get your stuff and leave." Iris knew more than anyone how much her friend had agonized over the changes she'd been going through about her sexuality. None of this had been easy for her.

"I don't think she's a traitor," Chrisanne said. "I'm just asking." She shrugged, the see-through white blouse that showed off a lacy black bra and propped up C-cups temporarily distracting Iris from why she was so pissed.

Imani cut her eyes at the girl and the rest of the bridesmaids looked so much like swans with ruffled feathers that Iris worried for a minute they would peck Chrisanne's eyes out.

"It's all right," Aisha said. "For real. She's not saying anything I haven't heard over the last few years."

But none of the women relaxed. They all looked at Chrisanne like the interloper she was. Just the day before, she'd come down from Florence where she'd been hanging with some American friends who had a summer home in the city. According to the conversation Iris overheard, Chrisanne saw Aisha's Facebook status updates about Italy and invited herself down, saying she was bored with her friends and their aggressively bougie ways. Which was saying something since Iris thought Chrisanne was the most bougie woman she'd ever met. San Pellegrino with every meal. No potential girlfriend who made below a certain amount of money. No natural hair. And certainly no one who couldn't afford to travel with her on her mandatory two foreign trips per year. All three of those criteria knocked Iris firmly out of the running, but she never considered herself a candidate for the position anyway. She narrowed her eyes at the twenty-six year old.

She was rude and didn't give a damn about anybody's feelings. Too bad she was sexy, and so very hard to ignore.

Chrisanne tilted her head to look at Iris. Her hair, straightened and thick, rippled over her shoulders. She frowned when she caught Iris' gaze.

Iris turned away and tuned back into the conversation on the terrace in time to hear Aisha say, "I'm still bi, Chrisanne. Just because Marco and I are together doesn't stop me from being attracted to women."

"So will you be in an open relationship or something?" Chrisanne knocked back the last of her martini and settled the empty glass on the table with a clack of glass on glass. "I can't imagine giving up the pussy, no matter how fine my man is."

"You don't even *want* a man," Imani muttered, eyeing Chrisanne from over the edge of her champagne glass.

Hands braced on the stone balcony on either side of her hips, Chrisanne leaned in to say something.

That's it. Iris cut her off. "I think you've said enough about this for the day."

She stood up and fluffed out the wide skirt of her dress. The cotton stuck to her thighs in the heat but she would never be ready to change it in favor of shorts and a tank top like Aisha and the bridesmaids had. The red and white cherry-patterned dress was vintage 1950's and belled out around her hips, emphasizing instead of detracting from her femininity. She wore her natural hair in a pompadour like Janelle Monáe, a look she'd discovered years ago and stuck with because it made her feel pretty.

"The party is in a couple of hours and I think Aisha should rest up for it." Iris glanced at her friend who looked a little tired but also a little tipsy. Nothing a disco nap couldn't fix. "Come on, honey." She put a hand on Aisha's shoulder. "Go take a nap. I'll wake you when it's time to get ready for the party."

She didn't wait for Aisha to agree, just helped her to her feet and pointed her through the wide French doors and toward her room. Once Aisha left, Imani gave up her appearance of not giving a fuck.

"Bitch, control yourself." She stood up to confront Chrisanne, hands propped on her hips like she was ready to grab the Vaseline and snatch off her earrings. "That's our friend out there," Imani said. "This is her wedding. Don't make her uncomfortable by bringing up shit she's already dealt with."

Chrisanne didn't look worried, although in her pastel blue romper and high heels she didn't look able to defend herself against Imani's pointed aggression. "Aisha and I talked about this before. She knows I'm just playing devil's advocate. You all are the ones getting your panties in a bunch. She's fine."

"You're missing the point." Iris fluffed her skirt again, encouraging the breeze to blow over her faintly damp thighs.

"And what point is that?" Chrisanne showed no signs of backing down.

"Aisha lost a lot of friends when she came out as bi. You asking her all those questions makes it seem like you'll be another one of those."

Imani narrowed her eyes at Chrisanne. "*Are* you one of those?"

Chrisanne sucked her teeth. One hundred percent Jamaican in that moment. "I don't give a shit who she fucks. I'm still her friend and we still have fun. She knows I'm just trying to satisfy my curiosity."

"Well, don't satisfy it at her expense," Iris said. "That's not what she needs right now."

Chrisanne shrugged. "Fine. Cool. I won't ask any more *awkward* questions." She looked meaningfully at Iris before she picked up a pale pink sweater and left the terrace in a clack of high heels.

Imani stared at Chrisanne's departing back like she wanted to set it on fire. "Why is she even here anyway?"

Iris shrugged. She had nothing to say when that was the very same question she wanted to ask.

Chapter 2

The evening's lavish pamper party went off without a hitch. Iris had arranged for nail techs and masseuses to come to their villa overlooking the sea for an evening of hors d'oeuvres, champagne, and pampering intended to leave Aisha and her bridesmaids boneless with relaxation. Everyone else coming to the wedding would arrive in three days, staying for the ceremony and the day after it while Aisha and her new husband went off on a yacht for their honeymoon. When the other forty guests came, it would be a madhouse.

For now, the villa was almost deserted, with the nighttime sounds of the sea whispering at them from below the cliffs and the perpetual and haunting sound of a Spanish guitar from one of the nearby houses. Aisha's fiancé, Marco, had rented the villa and its league of servants for the bridal party. He and his groomsmen were at a smaller villa on Capri, indulging in all the things that bachelors did before binding themselves to one person for the rest of their lives. Iris had been shocked at his generosity but Aisha had barely blinked.

It was luxury of the type Iris was not used to. Her job as an executive assistant at an Atlanta law firm did not allow her the extravagance of Italian villas, nearly invisible maids, and breakfast prepared by a chef in the mornings while she slept.

This was going to be Aisha's life now. An irony since her friend had always insisted she could take care of herself and had never wanted any of her stud girlfriends to take care of her. Her fiancé, a gorgeous Cameroonian man who had made his fortune in France and was now settled in London, insisted she have everything her heart desired. And she let him provide that for her.

At the pamper party, Iris avoided Chrisanne. She noticed that the little opportunist enjoyed the pampering as much as Aisha did, getting multiple colors on her nails, rejecting one after another while the nail tech eyed her with annoyance. Well, maybe she wasn't avoiding her as much as she should. After the party, she walked a very relaxed Aisha back to her room at the end of the hallway before going back to her own.

Iris closed her room door behind her with a soft click. In the dark, a gray light flickered at the bedside table and a low buzzing filled the room. Her phone. She hesitated, pressing her lips together in thought, before swiping a finger across the screen to accept the call.

"Hey." She stood near the bedside lamp and tapped her finger against the patterned silk lampshade, but did not turn on the light.

A voice tight with anger spat at her from the phone. "You been avoiding me?"

Iris sank into the padded chair near the bed and kicked off her shoes. The open window let in the salt-tinged air off the sea and she breathed it in with a low sigh. Although she'd only been at the villa for two days, she would miss it when she went back to Atlanta. The peace. The beauty. "Why would I be avoiding you, Jasmyn?"

"Because I wanted to talk to you, of course," Jasmyn answered.

If Iris had thought about it, she would have avoided talking to her almost-ex. Jasmyn was playing the attentive girlfriend now that Iris was halfway around the world, a role she never could successfully play while they were in the same city, or in the same apartment.

Jasmyn gave a sigh of her own through the telephone and, by the sound, Iris could tell she was about to get on a roll. She left the chair, pushed open the French doors, and walked out onto the terrace. Even in the darkness of night, the Amalfi Coast was almost too beautiful to be real. When Aisha first told her where the wedding was and that she was paying for the entire bridal party to travel to and stay at a villa, she hadn't been able to pack her things fast enough. And now that she was here, it broke her spirit a little to think about leaving. But she knew she'd break her wallet trying to stay on her own.

"Ever since you got over there, it seems like you have more important things to do than talk to me."

"Why would I spend my days on the phone when I'm here for Aisha? Besides, you're the one who said you needed more space. As far as I remember, 'space' doesn't mean calling someone every day." Especially since it had been three months since Jasmyn asked for "a break" from their relationship and stopped sleeping at their shared condo every night.

"I'm trying to reconnect with you." Jasmyn's voice deepened with calculated seduction. She was changing her approach. "Why won't you let me?"

Iris dropped heavily into the deck chair and tilted her head to gaze up at the starry sky. The Spanish guitar played on, slow and melancholy. Not for the first time, she wondered who was playing and what they were thinking. "Because I don't believe you," she said to Jasmyn. "You can't tell me one day you need a break and can't sleep in our bed anymore, then as soon as I'm thousands of miles away, you suddenly need to hear my voice. That doesn't make any sense."

"Why are you so damn suspicious, Iris? You're so much like a dude that way."

As if men had a monopoly on suspicion. A muscle ticked in Iris' jaw. "Don't start, Jasmyn."

"What? I'm just talking about your attitude, nothing else."

But she knew it wasn't true. They both did. Jasmyn had known every relevant thing about Iris before they started. Before they slept together, before they even went on their first official date. It was only later, months into their relationship, that she started making sly comments and hurtful innuendos. And those comments hadn't fully stopped in the two years they'd been together. Iris was finally sick of it.

"What do you really want?" she asked.

It could have been any number of things Jasmyn wanted. Although by now, Iris knew *she* wasn't one of those things. Not really. Jasmyn was polyamorous. She didn't tell Iris until late into their relationship when she wanted to bring other people into their lives and into their bed. Iris wasn't into that. Either it was going to be her and her girlfriend, or her alone.

When she said that, Jasmyn didn't think she was serious. She thought Iris would cave and give in like so many women had before, women who Iris was just now finding out about.

"You need to come to your senses," Jasmyn said. "It's not like you're going to find anyone who can deal with all your…issues."

Iris pressed her lips together and counted slowly to ten. "If I can't find anyone else to deal with my so-called issues then I guess it's better off for me to be alone."

"Fuck...you know I didn't mean it like that?"

"Like what? That it would be damn near impossible for me to find someone else? After two years together, is that what you think, Jasmyn? That no one else would want me?"

"God damn it! You're always blowing things out of proportion."

At nearly forty years old, Iris had managed to conquer *most* of her insecurities, but not all. When Jasmyn was being an asshole, those insecurities were what she attacked first—Iris' lingering doubts about who she was in the world, her worry that she wasn't like most lesbians.

And just then, she realized why Jasmyn had called. It wasn't to "reconnect." No, it was to push an argument so she could justify what they had become to each other. Nothing. Iris slumped in the chair, suddenly feeling a bone-deep exhaustion.

"Jaz. You said you wanted space." Her voice broke as the reality of what was happening finally became clear. They were truly over. "Please take it. Please take all the space and time you want. I'm done." She stood up and walked to the railing, the tiles warm under her bare feet, the soothing guitar building in speed until the melancholy bled away and it was a strumming invitation to a dance that floated from the house. But it was a dance Iris couldn't be part of.

Through a haze of tears, she stared past the tumbling vines of purple bougainvillea that looked nearly black in the darkness, the tall columns propping up the neighboring house on the hillside, its wide terrace facing the sea. Iris squeezed her eyes shut. In Atlanta, she'd practically begged Jasmyn to give their relationship another chance, told her not to rush their breakup, that she would consider role playing, visiting sex clubs with her, nearly anything that would give her girlfriend the variety she craved. Anything except taking in another lover.

Now, Iris was done begging for what should have already been hers.

"I'll talk to you when I get back, Jasmyn. We can work everything out then. Okay?"

"No." Jasmyn's answer was quiet. Final. "There's nothing to work out. You've made your decision and now I have to make mine."

Iris drew in a hissing breath. Deep inside, she ached to promise Jasmyn *anything* if she stayed. "Do what you need to do," she said instead.

"I will," her ex replied before hanging up.

Iris dropped the phone away from her ear. This pain was something she should have gotten used to by now, the feeling that the person she loved didn't think she was enough. But it was a hard knot under her breast bone. Yes, she was done. But that didn't make the pain disappear. Iris turned to go back inside and froze.

Chrisanne stood on the neighboring terrace, a look on her face that Iris could not decipher. Then a smirk replaced that look, an insulting twist of lips and the tilt of her eyebrows. Chrisanne nodded once at her and turned away to slip inside her room, leaving the afterimage of her smirk behind.

You total and absolute bitch!

Iris turned away from Chrisanne's empty balcony and closed her eyes, desperate to feel even a hint of the dancing lightness plucking merrily from the neighbor's guitar. But only sadness found her in the darkness behind her closed lids. She gripped the marbled edge of the terrace and leaned into the night, releasing a slow breath while the evening breeze brushed over her face. She was *so* over being sad.

Fiona Zedde

Chapter 3

"Where did you even find this bitch?" Iris smoothed sunscreen into her shoulders, frowning at the already browning and warm skin. She probably waited too long to apply the lotion.

After she was satisfied with her protection from skin cancer, she lay back down on the beach chair next to Aisha. A few feet away, waves tumbled up on the pebbly beach then retreated back into the sea with a sibilant whisper.

Aisha laughed and rolled over on her back, bits of sand, remnants of her earlier swim, clung to her skin, pale against dark, as she moved. "I met her at a friend's house in Naples a few years ago. She's crazy as hell, but fun. Don't let her smart mouth turn you off. She's almost a sweetheart under all that bullshit." Aisha smoothed a hand over her micro-braids, tucking them more firmly into the tight bun.

"You actually like her?"

Aisha laughed again. "Yes, I do."

Iris shrugged. "Okay then. If you like her, then the least I can do is not kill her before your wedding."

"I appreciate that."

Iris relaxed on her chair, listening to the sound of the waves, the kids playing nearby and the teenagers shouting as they body-surfed the high waves. This was as far from Atlanta as she could get and still be on this plane of existence. No traffic. The smell of sunscreen and the salt-tinged air. No one telling her she wasn't good enough.

Iris rolled over to her stomach to give her back some sun, adjusting the skirt of her bathing suit over her butt and the tops of her thighs. She rested her cheek on her arms and peeked down the beach. The bridesmaids were playing volleyball a safe distance away while Chrisanne made friends with a group of Italian women playing in the waves. Wearing a tiny white bikini, she splashed and ran into the sea, a big grin on her face. Her flirtatious laughter rippled across the beach.

Aisha stirred beside her. "Remember a few years ago when I was freaking out after realizing I was bi?"

"Yeah." Iris dragged her gaze away from Chrisanne and the tiny bikini bottoms slowly creeping between her ass cheeks. "I do remember."

She'd had her job at the law firm barely a week when Aisha called her late one night to tell her that, after living her life as a lesbian for twenty years, she thought she might be bisexual.

Aisha cried in her ear, got angry with herself, worried about what the lesbian community she'd been part of since high school would think of her if she started dating men. They talked until six the next morning when Iris had to get off the phone and get ready for work. After the call, Aisha sent a text to say she felt relieved that Iris had accepted her, that she now felt unburdened. But Iris felt like the load of Aisha's confession had dropped squarely on her shoulders. Would other lesbians think she was bisexual by association too? Almost six years later, she was embarrassed she'd made Aisha's revelation about her.

"I remember," Iris said again when Aisha didn't say anything else.

Aisha adjusted the dark glasses on her face. "I met Chrisanne at a friend's house around that time. I was traveling in Naples and she was just there, a stranger. And so damn young. I told her about the bi thing and she just shrugged like it was no big deal. She said that people changed, that it was almost impossible to stay the same as we grow older. Whether it's our sexuality or how we look or how we see the world." A smile flared to life on Aisha's face. "I hadn't heard that from anybody before. It was nice. After that, I started to come to terms with it myself and stop giving a fuck what people think."

That was a big step. They both had mutual friends who didn't speak to Aisha anymore. Some because, yeah, they were as bigoted as the straights. Others because they just didn't know what to say or how to interact with her anymore.

"I'm glad she was able to give you that." Iris said the words with as much sincerity as she could manage even though part of her burned with jealousy. No matter how hot that girl was—and Iris had to admit that she was *very* hot— she didn't want Chrisanne to usurp her place as Aisha's best lesbian friend.

"But she's not you." Aisha looked at Iris, smiling that serious smile of hers, one side of her mouth tucked up, her shades pushed to the top of her head to make sure Iris could see the sincerity in her eyes.

"Of course she isn't. Where else could you find another me?" Iris nudged Aisha with her foot, grinning.

Aisha's smile widened and she dropped the shades over her eyes, flopped back down onto her beach chair. Iris glanced over her shoulder to where Chrisanne ran through the waves with a short-haired woman. They both glistened from sunscreen and happiness, Chrisanne's slim and youthful body catching the eye of nearly everyone on the beach. Yeah, she was nice to look at but luckily Iris wasn't that shallow. She rested her head on the pillow of her arms and closed her eyes.

She was dozing off, falling into a light sleep when a splash of cold water jerked her up in the chair. "What the f—!"

Aisha jolted upright barely a foot away from Iris. "What happened?" She was perfectly dry, but Iris was dripping wet from the shoulders down, only her hair spared.

Iris blinked behind her shades to see Chrisanne with an empty bucket, standing over her with a mischievous look on her face. "You're not so perfect now, are you?"

Her voice was a tease, sing song and light, but there was something serious behind it, an intention that Iris couldn't let go of. She jumped up from the chair, almost falling. Chrisanne shrieked and dropped the bucket. She took off and Iris chased her. Chrisanne ran between the bodies reclined on the beach, children building sandcastles, topless sunbathers with their books or headphones.

"I am going to *kill* you!" Iris screamed.

She was cold. Her hair was wrapped up in a headscarf and dry, but her body had been shocked into full wakefulness and she wanted someone to pay. Under her running feet, the already meager sand gave way to rocks and the jagged beginning of a cliff, but Chrisanne still kept running. The rocks stabbed into Iris' feet. She stopped running with a cry of pain, glaring at Chrisanne who crowed with victory nearly twenty feet away.

"You need to run around barefoot in the country and get tough feet like me," she called out, flashing her smile.

She didn't seem like someone who grew up running around barefoot in anybody's country. Her hair was loose and long around her shoulders, salon-straight, her slim yet curvaceous body unselfconsciously displayed in the bright white bikini. She laughed and stomped playfully on the rocks, kicking up her feet to show Iris their tough soles.

"You're dead when I see you later," Iris muttered as she walked backwards to cool off her feet in the water. Damn, those rocks hurt.

"You're such a prissy chick," Chrisanne said with a wide grin. "One day you'll loosen up." Her eyebrow arched. "Maybe."

"If I ever do, you're not the one I'll do it with." Iris was pissed. Not just about the cold water on her back but about Chrisanne eavesdropping on her conversation, and the way the young girl talked to Aisha. She didn't spare Chrisanne another look as she turned and walked back down the beach.

When she sat down on the chair next to a perfectly dry Aisha, her friend put a hand on her shoulder. "You okay?"

"Yeah, sure," she said with the conviction of someone who was really *not* 'okay.' "Why wouldn't I be?"

Down the beach, Chrisanne had gone back to playing with her friends. She looked like she didn't have a single care in the world.

Chapter 4

Hours later, sun-drunk and browned from a day on the beach, Iris trudged up the steep path back up to the villa with Aisha, Chrisanne, and the bridesmaids. Except for those tense moments with Chrisanne, it had been a good afternoon. They'd eaten great Italian food on the sand then took a break from the hot sun to swim out to a yacht owned by a friendly neighbor.

Now, Iris' skin was tight and hot from the combination of sunscreen and the day's heat, drying seawater and the vague irritation of the skirt of her bathing suit against her thighs. She wanted to get naked and get clean.

Aisha tiredly kissed her cheek and made her way down the hall toward her room, already getting out her phone to call her fiancé. Imani and the other bridesmaids fanned out behind Aisha toward their own rooms, fighting yawns and wishing everyone else a good evening. Dinner wasn't for another hour or so. Iris had a suspicion everyone would take most of that time to nap.

She adjusted her beach bag over her shoulder and turned toward her room.

"Hey."

Iris stopped with her hand on her door handle and considered not turning around. But Chrisanne called out to her again, her voice sharper, demanding the attention Iris didn't want to give.

Iris turned. "What's up?" She kept her voice carefully neutral.

"Are you pissed at me about today?"

"What about today?" Iris's spine stiffened. She didn't know what Chrisanne was up to and didn't really care.

"Don't be a bitch. You know what I mean. The water."

Iris flinched as if she felt the cold water douse her back again. That flash of unexpected cold, wetness flooding her bathing suit, running down her back and down the sides of her breasts, down over her ass. Chasing away all the warmth of the sun.

"You and I don't play like that." Iris crossed her arms over her chest, dangling the beach bag from a clenched fist. There wasn't much in the bag. Sunglasses. Her book. A beach towel and the flip flops she'd forgotten to put on when she chased Chrisanne down the beach.

Chrisanne mirrored her position. She was going to say something, and Iris could tell it wasn't nice. But Chrisanne pressed her lips together and dropped her defensive stance. "I'm sorry about listening to your private conversation the other night. I didn't mean to."

Iris had hoped that was one conversation they wouldn't have, that they could just pretend Chrisanne hadn't overheard her humiliating phone call with Jasmyn.

"Are you really sorry though?" she asked.

"Let me fucking apologize, damn it. You don't always have to be so prickly all the time."

"Okay, fine then. I accept your apology." Iris rolled her eyes, sure this was the first time someone had ever given her such an aggressive so-called apology. "What were you doing out there anyway?" As soon as she asked the question, she knew it was stupid.

What would Chrisanne be doing on the balcony outside her own damn room? Whatever the hell she wanted, obviously. "Never mind."

The corners of Chrisanne's mouth twitched. "I wasn't out there to listen in on you."

"But you listened anyway."

"I couldn't very well ignore it."

Iris sighed. This conversation was going nowhere. "Listen. I feel really dirty and I just want to shower this sand off me. Can we talk about this some other time?"

"Sure. How about after your shower? I'm about to get clean too. Something tells me that everyone else is pretty much done for the day."

She didn't want to talk about whatever it was Chrisanne had on her mind. But she agreed to the conversation anyway. "Just give me about half an hour," she said. So much for a long and relaxing evening lying naked under the ceiling fan.

It took her about forty minutes to shower. Under the spray, she couldn't help but wonder what Chrisanne wanted. Why the younger woman seemed so intent on talking about something that wasn't worth mentioning. She was getting on Iris' nerves, but so what? She was getting on everyone's nerves and Iris didn't see her trying to make up to any of the other women because of it.

When Iris opened her eyes from under the water, pushing her thick wet hair back off her face and down her neck, she realized how long she'd been in the shower. She quickly rinsed off and climbed out.

She was sitting on the bed, smoothing lotion into her skin when a knock sounded on her door. The clock said nearly an hour had passed since she left Chrisanne in the hallway. Iris quickly finished rubbing the lotion between her toes and slipped on the dress she'd pulled out to wear. It was thin and white, with a flared skirt and black polka dots. Her usual style but thin enough for a summer in southern Italy without getting heatstroke. She adjusted the lace collar in the mirror before grabbing her purse and slipping into her shoes.

Chrisanne had lifted her hand to knock again when Iris opened the door. "Ready?"

Chrisanne gawked at her for a moment, blinking as she looked Iris up and down. She cleared her throat and dropped her hand. "Yes, I am." She cleared her throat again and put her hands in the pockets of her slim fitting Capri slacks. A thin white blouse with a plunging neckline gave her look a chic movie star edge. "Would you like to go out for a drink?"

Iris looked down at her dress, glad she'd erred on the side of "pretty" instead of casual, and shrugged. "Sure." She slipped her key to the villa in her purse and closed the door behind her. "Lead the way."

Like her, Chrisanne was wearing highly inappropriate shoes. High heeled pumps that clacked like music against the tile floors, a sound that Iris loved. The way they walked together, unconsciously falling into the same rhythm, made her feel like she was in a Gina Lollobrigida film, skirt swinging around her knees, the sound of the neighbor's guitar warming up for the evening.

Their breaths puffed as they climbed the steep road together, the climb pinching Iris' feet but not enough for her to regret her high heels. Chrisanne walked ahead of her to push open a door nearly hidden by drooping white bougainvillea and bursts of purple flowers that Iris hadn't noticed in the waning light.

The faint scent of fresh lemons poured out of the little restaurant, an odd and hungering flavor. Her twin, Ian, said the smell of lemons made him want to clean not eat. There was some sort of statement about their personalities in that, but Iris never bothered to follow through with the idea.

The restaurant-bar was small, only a half dozen tables, most of them occupied. But Chrisanne took the last table near the window, flickering her eyes around the room, her hands smoothing the material of her slacks over her thighs as she sat down. The waitress brought a bottle of red wine without taking their order first, smiling with her whole body at Chrisanne. A smile that spoke of more than casual familiarity.

"You've been around," Iris said.

The look Chrisanne gave her was not kind, but she still poured wine for them both and sat back to drink from the sturdy goblet.

"Only to the most fun places," Chrisanne said after a swallow of wine. Her eyes snapped with a fire Iris was getting to know intimately from close up.

Iris put the wine glass to her lips and let the warm Chianti linger on her tongue before swallowing it down, slowly. It wasn't from an impulse to savor the wine, but rather to stall when she would have to talk. She didn't know what to say to Chrisanne. They were as far apart as the earth and stars, and just as likely to find a way to co-exist in close proximity. Finally, she swallowed her wine and licked her lips.

"What do you want?" Iris didn't bother to hide her impatience with the whole thing. Sure, she had put on outside clothes and walked willingly with this near-stranger up a dark mountainside in a part of Italy she had never been, but that was just about all she was willing to do. As if that wasn't enough.

A look of surprise hijacked Chrisanne's face, the red O of her mouth gaping while she stared at Iris, blinking. "I want to talk. Can't I just buy you a glass of wine in apology? I told you I'm—" She stopped. "You know what? Never mind. Just drink your damn wine. When you're done, I'll walk you back to the house. We don't have to say anything to each other." But she didn't seem capable of following her own recommendation. She hissed in a breath that may have meant to be calming but it left her looking even more irritated than before. "Where the fuck do you get off—?" Her lashes whipped the air as if she was blinking against a windstorm. "—walking around here all judgmental, like butter wouldn't melt in your mouth…"

Iris settled her wine glass carefully on the table. This wasn't the first time she was hearing something like this, other women misinterpreting her quietness, assuming she was looking down her nose at them when she wasn't looking at them at all.

Chrisanne sat across from her with an expectant gaze. Like she was waiting for Iris to say something even more cutting to her. But Iris only drained the last of her wine before signaling for Chrisanne to refill her glass.

"Aren't you the one being judgmental here?"

Iris made the statement with the absolute certainty that Chrisanne would say something ridiculous that showed her selfishness and lack of awareness of the people around her.

"I don't act like I have a stick up my ass," Chrisanne said. "My own shortcomings are much more boring. I overcompensate for my shyness with inappropriate comments and ill-timed sexual jokes. Everyone knows that."

"Everyone who knows you, I'm assuming."

"And you don't put yourself in that number? Shocking. Aren't you the type to assume you know all about me?" She refilled Iris' glass with a twist of her mouth, topped off her own and knocked back a fair amount of the sharp red wine. The red stained her lower lip, a full and wet curve that Iris unfortunately noticed. "Why do you think you're better than everyone?" Chrisanne asked.

"You're assuming that I even *think* about everyone." Iris sipped her wine as her words came more freely.

The girl was getting more...predictable with each word, more open. So much so that it didn't really matter what Iris said to her, she would still sit there and judge and assume

27

and carry right on making everyone else uncomfortable. This was the kind of personality she could easily deal with. She had enough experience with similar types at her job where she had to deal with rich people who didn't care about anything but their bottom line.

Iris drank more of her wine. The restaurant's small size was appealing in that as soon as they reached near the end of the bottle, another one appeared. Then a small basket of warm bread, butter, meats and cheeses. Chrisanne had ordered none of it.

Chrisanne buttered a piece of bread and took a tentative bite. She chewed and swallowed. "What if I told you that I've been Aisha's friend longer than you?"

"I'd say it doesn't matter," Iris shrugged. "Then I'd say you're lying."

Chrisanne pursed her lips, as if she was tasting the words waiting to fall out of her mouth. "I know you dumped her when she first came out as bi."

Iris nearly bit her tongue in two. No one knew that. At least no one else besides her and Aisha. Iris had voiced her support for her friend when she declared her bisexuality, but she'd been shocked, and annoyed that "yet another dyke" was going straight just to be respectable.

It had felt like a betrayal since she and Aisha had come out together in college. Had gone through some of the same struggles. Had told their parents together and had chosen to live in Atlanta because of its big gay and lesbian population. She was only thinking what others in the community did.

After the "bi revelation," she still hung out with Aisha, had girls' nights out and did everything they'd done in the past. But for Iris, the experience had soured. She didn't think she had anything in common with Aisha anymore. Or at least that's what she thought. Years of that went by.

Eventually, her betrayal got back to Aisha, as things like that inevitably do. The look on Aisha's face had been devastating.

They were good friends, best friends even, but never made a habit of talking about feelings and other things that really mattered. If anyone asked Iris, she would've simply said she and Aisha had grown apart. One moment they were friends and the next, the phone calls stopped being exchanged, and then it became one year then three since they'd spoken.

Unlike what Chrisanne said, it hadn't been a "dumping" when Aisha came out. It was worse than that. She'd led her friend to think they were still friends, when in reality she'd abandoned her.

It had taken a mutual friend and an organized trip to northern Italy where Aisha and Iris were tossed together. They managed to avoid each other for most of the week, then a hard and unexpected rain trapped them together on a tiny boat in the middle of the lake. They'd been uncomfortable. Then bored enough to talk. Then confess. Then forgive. It was the reason Iris loved Italy so much. It was not only the place she'd traveled to on her first trip abroad. It was also the place that had given Iris her friend back.

She looked over her nearly empty wine glass at Chrisanne. "You don't know anything about me."

The woman had the nerve to laugh. Well, sort of giggle as she leaned across the table, elbows wobbling from the effort of holding her torso up. Her drunken torso.

"By the time you 'got her back'—" She put her wine glass down long enough to make air quotes. "—I had been friends with her at least two years already. All the time you lost being a small minded little bitch. Don't think she didn't tell me about you."

Iris winced at the thought that she'd hurt Aisha enough for her to talk about their relationship with this girl, a near stranger.

"Don't take everything you hear about other people as truth," Iris said.

Chrisanne rolled her eyes. "If anything, she was generous about you."

Iris could believe that. Aisha had always been kind. Even to the person who was twisting the knife in her back.

The failures of her past never failed to make her cringe. Of anyone, she should've been the person offering Aisha unconditional support. She should've been the one there for Aisha through dick and pussy and everything in between that she wanted to put her mouth on. Iris jerked her train of thought to a standstill. Wait. When did she even think like that? She frowned at the nearly empty second bottle of wine. She licked her lips and tasted the sweetness of the grapes there, hints of the gorgonzola cheese she had nibbled on during their painful but strangely easy conversation. Iris crossed her legs under her crinoline skirts and sat up straight in the chair, determined to look the very opposite of what was now painfully obvious to her.

"I think I'm drunk," she said.

Chrisanne gave her a crooked version of her usual smile. "Of course you are. I would be insulted if you weren't."

Iris wrinkled her nose as she gave up on her military straight posture, whatever that really meant. The curve of her spine hit the back of the chair and her legs stretched out under the table until the toe of one stiletto touched what she assumed was Chrisanne's chair. She tapped at it in irritation. The Chianti had been unusually good and the little cheese and meat plate was the perfect thing to break up the wet spice of the wine.

"Is that your plan?" Iris asked. "To get me drunk enough to confess things you have no business knowing?"

"Aisha is my business. Although you don't think so, she's a good friend. She is always kind to me when everybody else treats me like the stepsister who writes bad checks, or worse."

Iris could easily imagine the "worse." Chrisanne was a little bit of a slut, if the past few days' interaction was anything to go by. She flirted with anything in a skirt and made friends every place they went. Despite seeming to deliberately cultivate the bridesmaids' hatred, Chrisanne was charming to strangers. And she wasn't an ugly woman.

Iris moved to tap her shoe against the chair again but encountered soft flesh instead. She slid her stiletto off and

31

rubbed apologetically at the injured leg with her bare foot. "That's hard for me to believe since sometimes you don't really act like it." Chrisanne gave her a slightly dazed look, like she was losing the thread of the conversation. "Like Aisha is a good friend," Iris clarified.

Chrisanne sucked her teeth and seemed to get herself together. "Fuck you, Lucy Ricardo." She signaled the waitress for another bottle of wine.

After the new bottle was uncorked and poured by the same flirtatious waitress, Chrisanne grabbed it, picked up her glass and walked with a surprisingly steady gait toward a door at the back of the restaurant. "Come on!" she said over her shoulder. Iris slid on her shoe and followed.

It was a balcony; wide enough for maybe four people to share comfortably. The railing and half the restaurant's outer wall crawled with some sort of bright yellow flowers and thick vines. At least Iris assumed they were a vivid yellow. In the dark, they were a faded cream, but she imagined in the daylight they would rival the sun in brightness.

With her wine glass held in a loose grip, she leaned over the balcony at Chrisanne's side. The balcony looked down on the backyard of a decent-sized villa, its vine-covered rear gate and a hint of blue that must have been the pool. Privacy for both the observer and the observed.

"You know what's the really messed up part of this whole entire shit?'

The question must have been rhetorical because Chrisanne plunged on without giving Iris time to reply. "I wish you were a fucking ridiculous redhead with unnecessary words and bug eyes." She turned to lean back against the balcony, the wine lifted to her mouth. "You're more like Dorothy Dandridge or even Eartha Kitt…yeah. You have that undeniable sense of who you are that makes everyone else want to be you or want to fuck you." Chrisanne's gaze fluttered down Iris' body and Iris felt it like a touch. "You're so hot that I literally *ache* every time I look at you."

Iris put her wine on the table and pressed back against the closed door between the balcony and the rest of the bar. Through the wooden door, she heard the music of the restaurant, vague hums of conversation, the thump of glass on wood. Despite the drunken clouds floating through her head, she knew she didn't want to take this where Chrisanne apparently wanted it to go. "You know this is not a good idea."

"What? I just made a simple statement." Chrisanne's mouth glistened from the wine, a wet rosebud. Moonlight slid between the clouds, seeking out every thick strand of hair in Chrisanne's elegant up-do, silvering the curves of her full-lipped face.

"I'm not one of your easy fucks, Chrisanne. Getting on my back for you isn't something that I'll ever do."

"Who says I want you on your back?" Her mouth gleamed wet and filthy in the moonlight. Slutty had never been Iris' style and she wasn't about to start now.

But she couldn't stop staring at Chrisanne's mouth, or the way the slacks fit just so to her rounded hips, how her pose against the railing—one leg stretched out and the other with the knee raised—emphasized the sheer femininity of her. She didn't want to notice any of these things.

"Do you ever stop?" Iris asked. A familiar warmth was beginning to pool in her belly. A poisonous arousal that wasn't going to end with anything good.

Chrisanne licked her wine stained lips. "Only if you tell me to."

"I want you to stop now." Iris was deadly serious in that moment, no games, and drunken fog be damned.

Chrisanne caught on to her tone pretty quickly. She smiled lazily and pulled her wandering gaze back to Iris' face. "You're no fun," she said.

"What is this?" Iris asked. "Why are we here?"

Chrisanne's eyes drifted just right of Iris' face then back. "The other night." Her voice roughened, although Iris couldn't tell if it was from emotion or the drinks. "On your balcony when you were talking to your...whatever. I should have gotten up and left or at least let you know I was there. It was a bullshit move for me not to at least apologize right after you saw me. I was just...too embarrassed to be caught hearing your business."

She'd been embarrassed? Iris distinctly remembered being the one crying and carrying on like Jasmyn was ripping the very fabric of her life apart. Even now, heat flickered under her face at the memory of the raw pleading she'd almost subjected all three of them to.

"Did it get you off to see me like that?" She crossed her arms and leaned even more into the door. "Did you think I got what I deserved, the stuck up bitch who always looks down her nose at other people?"

"It wasn't that," Chrisanne murmured. "You shouldn't have to beg. Either someone loves you or they don't. If they don't, your begging makes them hate you a little." She looked annoyed with herself for saying that much. "Shit...sometimes I talk too much."

Her words sounded like painful experience. That softened something inside Iris. But only a little. "In vino veritas, and all that," Iris muttered.

"What?"

"Drunks tell the truth."

"I'm not a drunk," Chrisanne held her forehead in an exaggerated wrinkle. "Just inebriated."

Iris was impressed Chrisanne managed to say the word right. She wasn't sure if her own tongue was that capable just then.

Her drinks were fast catching up to her and the island of sobriety she'd found for a brief moment was suddenly no longer beneath her feet.

Across from her, Chrisanne put the nearly empty glass to her mouth and drained it. She put it on the railing, barely looking over her shoulder when it tilted and fell over the side. Iris heard a thump, the glass falling on dirt instead of hard pavement. She wondered how many glasses ended up under the balcony every day.

Her scattered wonderings abruptly stopped when Chrisanne crowded into her space, bringing the hot scent of wine and perfume and confrontation. "Come back to my room with me," she said.

"No."

But Iris' "no" quickly became a "yes," gasping from her swollen mouth between Chrisanne's rough kisses. Chrisanne wasn't graceful, or particularly subtle. One moment, she was on the other side of the balcony and unreasonably attractive—was it wine goggles?—and the next she was breathing her wine scented breath over Iris' lips, tempting and soft in her silk slacks.

Iris reached out, probably to steady Chrisanne from bumping into her and break both their noses and thus ruining Aisha's wedding, but her hands on Chrisanne's hips just steadied the slimmer woman, held her tight but leaving inches of necessary space between them, then they were kissing and she was tasting wine, a slick and skilled tongue, and pastrami she hadn't eaten.

"You taste good..."

She didn't know who said it. But it didn't matter. Chrisanne's hips under her hands felt sublime, rounded and perfect against her palms, the skin hot through her slacks.

Iris could think of at least a half dozen reasons not to do this. But between the hot suction of Chrisanne's mouth around her tongue and the girl's hands careful and tender on the small of her back, Iris lost every single one of those reasons to the slow river dripping between her legs.

"Let's pay and leave," Chrisanne said against her lips, voice rough, fingers never leaving the small of Iris' back. Something in that was more erotic than if she'd touched her anywhere else.

Iris could only whimper her agreement.

They left the restaurant under the wounded gaze of the waitress who wished, Iris knew, that she was in her place, and hurried down the hill to the villa. They didn't talk. There was no reason to. It was just the click of their shoes on the road, their anticipatory breathing, the smell of summer flowers in the air. That time should have given Iris the clarity to say no. But instead it only amplified her desire, made her want Chrisanne even more, made her lose every single shred of the common sense that she might have had.

Those minutes had her imagining the ways that she would have Chrisanne. Spread out on the bed with her blouse ripped from her shoulders and spilling out the thick fruit of her breasts. She thought, with heart-tripping pleasure, of the way Chrisanne would look under the lamplight coming through the curtains from the bedroom's balcony, the noises she would make when Iris kissed between her legs, the clench and quiver of her stomach muscles when she came.

Before they made it back to the villa, Iris had already had Chrisanne in a dozen different ways in her mind, and the pulse between her legs only throbbed for more.

The walk was relatively quick, or it felt that way with the things slipping and wriggling through Iris' thoughts.

Sex. Sex. Sex.

It shouldn't have been that way. She should be more careful. But she was so tired of careful and of having to do things the way other people wanted, easing herself into their lives in a way that was palatable to them. Sometimes, she just *wanted*. She wanted to take and be taken. The simplicity of a sexual transaction that had been denied to her all of her life. It was the bottle of red wine talking. It had to be. There was no other reason she was thinking and feeling this way.

At the villa, they paused in the long hallway leading to the bedrooms.

"Yours?" Chrisanne asked, breathless.

To answer, Iris nudged her further down the hallway toward the other room. Unlike hers, no one would likely come knocking on Chrisanne's door, asking for something related to the wedding. Iris didn't want to be interrupted. Not now, not tonight.

Chrisanne opened her door with a practiced twist of her wrist, pulled Iris into the dark room and shoved her back against the door. They kissed. More of an exchange of hot breath, tender lips bruising against teeth, a clumsy desperation that was at odds with what they had done on the restaurant's balcony.

Iris panted into Chrisanne's mouth, fingers digging into her waist. Someone was making desperate little noises, by the time she realized it was her, they had moved from the door to the bed. Chrisanne pushed her down into soft sheets, a hand at the back of Iris' neck to lift her mouth even more into her kisses. The flavor of wine was long gone. Licked and sucked away, leaving only the taste of Chrisanne, a fresh and crisp flavor on her tongue.

"You taste incredible, so fucking delicious."

When Chrisanne pulled her mouth away to gasp the words, Iris found herself smiling. That was one thing she never thought of this woman as, gentle and sweet, making her partner feel as good with words as she could with her hands and mouth. But then again, maybe that was why the women flocked back to her bed again and again.

"You're not what I expected," Iris said between kisses, aware of the slowing down of the frantic *now now now* in her blood. The sweetness from Chrisanne was like honey over her skin. She suspected the woman would know what she was doing in bed, but this, this unexpected attention to all parts of the seduction, made Iris weak.

Their kisses slowed even more. Or more precisely, she slowed her kisses and Chrisanne followed her lead, nipping lightly at her lips, licking into her mouth, pulling back to breathe before connecting again, their tongues twining against each other, a slick and sensuous dance that made Iris squirm against the sheets and ache for more contact. But she kept her thighs closed and tucked to the side. The skirt of her dress was a rustling wall of cotton and tulle between them, delaying that press of hips to hips that would take things further than they were both ready for. But she moaned into Chrisanne's mouth, enjoying the slide of their tongues, the slow eroticism of them moving against each other in the bed.

Iris didn't know when the slow became stop. Only that she felt the fluttering of Chrisanne's lashes against her cheek, her mouth's stillness which she answered with a stillness of her own. Then there was even more darkness, then sleep.

Chapter 5

The guitar's strum woke her well before dawn. Iris opened her eyes to darkness, the press of her clothes on her skin and the warmth of another body against hers. She stirred, memories of the last moments before sleep making her squirm.

Shit. I can't believe I fell asleep. Then. *Shit! I can't believe I let things get that far.*

A hand brushed her hip through the dress. "Are you awake?"

Chrisanne's morning breath brushed her face and Iris grimaced. But...

"Yes. That damn guitar."

"But isn't it beautiful?" Chrisanne's hand on her hip tightened.

They lay there in the gloom together, listening to the music of the guitar pouring through the open balcony doors. It was strange, lying with someone in the same bed after so long. It had been nearly four months since she and Jasmyn had taken a break. This waking together was nice. But dangerous too.

Iris turned to Chrisanne in the dark and the other woman's eyes were still on her. She wasn't smiling. But her gaze was intent and focused. Not on Iris' mouth or even her eyes, but drifting like a caress over her entire face. It made Iris squirm although for a different reason than minutes before. It was almost like—

"I want to fuck you," Chrisanne said.

41

Or maybe it wasn't what she thought. The guitar plucked at the twilight between them, making the fact of her lying with a stranger in an 18th century villa on the Italian coast seem like an entirely different reality from the one Iris knew. The reality where she knew the rules and was expected, by herself and everyone else, to follow them. This place was nothing like her real life, so here, everything was possible.

"Then fuck me," she said.

This time, she was the one who kissed, reaching out to grasp the back of Chrisanne's neck and bring her close. Chrisanne groaned something. Maybe a complaint about her morning breath, maybe even an appreciation for how quickly Iris got with the program. Either way, it didn't matter. Their lips were pressed together and the monster of their combined morning breath was no reason to stop either of them from getting what they wanted.

Their flame caught quickly, a flick of gasoline on a fire left to glow through the night. Iris hissed at the commanding curl of Chrisanne's fingers over her ribs. Their kiss was wet and deep, leading to another then another until they were both gasping in the bed and moving desperately against each other.

Chrisanne bent her head to kiss Iris' throat, the space between her collarbones, and lower. Iris shivered at the touch of the hot mouth on her skin, biting and licking its way south. Chrisanne paused, took a breath, the heat from her lips ghosting over Iris' skin. It had been so damn long since she'd had a lover touch her with such a mixture of tenderness and desire. Chrisanne's want was unmistakable, and that made Iris want to please her.

They hadn't managed to take their clothes off from the night before. They were both still fully dressed, Iris in her dress, Chrisanne in her slacks and blouse, but both of their shoes tumbled on the floor.

The rustling between them grew. Hands over cloth, breaths quickening, the wet sounds of their kisses.

Chrisanne pulled down the top of Iris' dress. Her breath huffed in her throat. Eyes wide with amazement as she stared at Iris' bared skin.

"Every part of you is fucking gorgeous," she said, breathless. "It's so damn unfair." She left pleasure in the wake of her touch down the sloping line to Iris' breasts. "But I'm not going to complain right now." Chrisanne lowered her head.

Iris groaned when the hot tongue licked her nipples, one after the other, warm breath puffing at her skin while Chrisanne cradled the curve of her ribs in both hands. She was being too careful.

Iris twisted her fingers in Chrisanne's hair and yanked her head back. "I won't break you know."

Chrisanne's eyes glittered. "That's good to know."

Her mouth was pink and wet, the remnants of her lipstick sticking stubbornly to her mouth and adding to the look of debauched beauty that made Iris want to fuck her mouth and come all over her face. It had been far too long since she got laid. Much longer than three months.

With glittering eyes, Chrisanne bent her head again and her teeth dug into Iris' nipples, lips dragging up her aching flesh in a firm suction.

Iris hissed. The way Chrisanne lapped at her nipples, tugging sweetly at the one not in her mouth, made her imagine the girl doing the same thing to her clit, lightly pinching her clit between her fingers and sucking her...

Arousal jerked hard through Iris' belly, muscles jumping, her body tightening and hardening in a way it hadn't in a very long time. Abruptly, she was right *there*. She yanked her hips back.

"Stop, stop, stop!" Iris gasped, her fingers clenching in the sheets. She was too close, an explosion that would stop everything before it properly got started. "Too fast, too good." She licked her lips and pulled away from Chrisanne to pant roughly at the ceiling. Chrisanne petted her waist, easing the zipper of her dress farther down.

"I'm only getting started, baby. If you want to come, it's okay." She licked Iris' ear, inciting shivers and goose bumps all over her arms and neck. "It's not like you're a guy and that'll be it for us. We can go as long as we want."

"I'm not sure I have more than one round in me, though." Iris rolled over to stop the hands tugging down her dress. "Maybe you do, but I'm older than I look."

She knew she should stop this for real, say more than she already had, but the lust had drained away her good sense. All she wanted was that fulfillment of the incendiary heat pooling in her belly. She wanted to come. She wanted to share pleasure. She wanted to fuck.

And so, she ignored the voice inside her head that sounded disturbingly like her brother and took Chrisanne's hand in hers. Carefully, she guided the girl's hand under her dress, past the edge of her panties, and to her pussy. A sigh fluttered from her throat when those slim fingers slipped into her wetness.

"Shit…you feel like heaven." Her breath shuddered as Chrisanne fucked her with sure fingers. Chrisanne moved, sliding deeper, her hand shifting to brush up against…

Iris shivered at the unintended stimulation and bucked her hips.

Chrisanne's eyes fluttered open in confusion. "Huh?" Her voice was lust-drunk. She jerked back. "Are you packing under there?" She panted and licked her lips, visibly pulling herself back together.

Shit. Right. Fuck.

Iris knew better. Maybe she'd become complacent in the two years since she'd been with Jasmyn and the three years before that of not sleeping with anybody. She carefully pulled her hips back and pulled down her skirt. Chrisanne didn't try to stop her.

"I'm not packing, no. Not exactly." Iris took a calming breath. "Usually I have a talk with a potential lover before getting to this point." She adjusted her skirt around her thighs and sat up.

"But that…" Chrisanne looked confused. "It felt warm, like actual skin. Is it real?"

"Yes."

Chrisanne blinked at Iris like she didn't understand what she just said. Then the gears in her head apparently started turning again. She jerked away from Iris, anger quickly replacing her shock.

"What the fuck?! I told you I'm a lesbian. I don't fuck with guys. I got over that shit years ago."

"I am *not* a man." Iris struggled to pull her mind and body back from that hot place. This was a conversation she was tired of having, even though she knew it was necessary. "I just happen to be a woman born with a penis and a vagina."

Her thighs trembled with nervousness under her dress, fluttering the belled skirt that was just like all the others she'd worn most of her adult life to disguise the line of her penis. Iris linked her fingers together and waited for what Chrisanne would say.

"Jesus. You really do want it all, don't you?" The bed squeaked as Chrisanne got up.

Iris made a noise of relief, glad that Chrisanne still could joke at a time like this. She apologized again. "I never thought we'd..." She gestured to their half-naked bodies.

"Are you serious? Did I have to spell out how much I wanted to fuck you?" Something she saw on Iris' face made Chrisanne roll her eyes. "I guess I had to. Apologies for not just showing you my pussy and telling you to lick it." She made another sound of frustration. "Fuck. You really know how to kill the mood, don't you?"

"Believe me, it's not on purpose. I'd much rather be eating your pussy than having any sort of conversation." Iris was annoyed at herself again for not doing the usual due diligence. But she didn't even know the girl was interested in her in that way. If anything, she thought Chrisanne was trying to take her place as Aisha's best lesbian friend. Her brother always said she was terrible at reading other people.

Iris climbed out of the bed, feeling uncomfortable just lying there with her pussy throbbing and wet, her dick half-hard while Chrisanne looked at her like she just boiled her bunny.

Okay, stop.

Her hormones were pushing her between one extreme and the other. This was just a potential fuck, for Christ's sake.

Iris pressed fingers to her temples, aware of the vague throb of a blossoming headache. "I think we should call it a night, don't you?"

Chrisanne startled like she'd been miles away. "Yeah. You're right." She took a deep breath, watched Iris zip up her dress and re-settle her skirt. "Does anyone else here know about this?"

Iris frowned. "What? That I have a real dick too or that we almost fucked tonight." She didn't hide her annoyance. Was she worried already that Iris would blow her real lesbian status out of the water?

"This is a lot." Chrisanne made a desperate motion toward Iris' hips, scooting back across the sheets. "I don't

47

deal with dicks. I haven't since I was young and stupid. And I'd like to think that was a long time ago."

Iris took a breath, deciding then and there she would give the girl a break. It was no one's fault but her own that they were in this situation in the first place. "Only Aisha knows about me," she said. "She's known since college."

"Okay." Chrisanne took another deep breath. "Okay," she said again and sat on the edge of her bed. "I'll uh…see you tomorrow."

"Okay. See you." Iris opened the door and escaped to her own room.

Behind her closed door, she released a deep breath. The guitarist continued playing and she went to the balcony doors, intending to shut him out. But the night brushed her overheated face with its soothing fingers and she stepped out to the balcony instead. She leaned on the stone railing and looked down at the illuminated boats floating on the water, the climbing staircase of lights in the houses on the hilltop. Her skirts whispered against her thighs, the scent of flowers and lemon blossoms teased the back of her throat. She swallowed the sweetness and closed her eyes.

Iris had come to terms with herself a long time ago. There had been no years of struggle, no fighting with her family over her fair share of love. Her parents, told in the beginning that they were expecting twin boys, adapted themselves when she was born. Both nurses, they saw to it that she hadn't been mutilated and gave her everything she needed as a child to thrive in the world. There was no battle to see where in gender she fit. Iris was female, had been born to be, despite what the doctors called ovotestes, the presence of both male and female genitalia. She'd read in a medical journal where they called it "ambiguous" genitalia, but there was nothing ambiguous about her four-inch penis or her vagina. She loved them both. But not everyone did.

The guitarist played on and Iris stood on the balcony listening to him, deliberately emptying her mind. She felt completely sober. Stone cold. Now, she knew the difference between a good idea and a really bad one. But it was already too damn late.

Chapter 6

The next morning, Iris woke too early with barely three hours of sleep behind her and a long day ahead. She cracked her eyes open to glare at her phone's clock then stumbled to the bathroom and brushed her teeth. She swallowed two aspirin with some water from the sink, took a cool shower, and left her room, barely dressed, in search of coffee and solitude. Instead of coffee, she found espresso. Instead of solitude, she found Chrisanne.

Iris froze, immediately regretting not throwing on something more substantial over her nightgown. But she couldn't very well turn around and walk back to her room. Her hand tightened around the small coffee cup.

Chrisanne lay stretched out on a lounge chair in the early morning sun, looking as wrecked as Iris felt. Eyes drooping and red. Body limp. But even obviously hung over, she was distractingly gorgeous. A piece of kente cloth was wrapped around her heavy hair and twisted into a high crown, while her face was bare of makeup, and a tiny tank top and matching shorts showed off her lean body. Iris had a flashback of the night before, Chrisanne hovering over her, nipples firm buds pressing through her thin shirt, her mouth swollen from their kisses. She blinked the image away and reluctantly made her way out to the balcony, tiny espresso cup and saucer in hand, and sat on the chair furthest away from Chrisanne.

Chrisanne spared her a sort of smile and looked back down into her own small cup. "I thought for sure you'd sleep late."

"I'm not much for sleeping late away from home," Iris said. "You?"

"I'm not much for sleeping late when I have things on my mind."

"Things?"

"Oh, please." Chrisanne rolled her eyes. "You were there last night. What *things* do you think I'm talking about?"

Jesus. Were they really going to have this conversation? "There's nothing to think about. I made a mistake not putting on the brakes sooner. I was an idiot last night. I shouldn't have tried to...you know."

"Fuck me?" A smile moved across Chrisanne's face, then left as quickly as it came. She sipped from her cup. The espresso must have been too hot because she winced and licked her lips. "So, this thing of yours..." Her voice drifted off but her eyes came back to rest firmly on Iris.

Iris pressed her lips together. *Yes, I guess we are going to have this conversation.* "So...what?"

The turn in conversation made her hyper-aware of what she was wearing. Usually when she left her room at this time of the morning, she was the only one up. Maybe a servant or two, but she normally had the run of the house until at least nine or ten when the bridesmaids started to stir. Sometimes Aisha woke before then, but if her friend did, it was nothing for Iris to wear her nightgown in front of her. Now she regretted the short peignoir, a barely thigh-high orange thing with a matching robe that she'd bought on a whim, thinking it was the perfect little bit of nothing to wear while laying around in an Italian villa. She mostly wore it on her balcony and on her early morning forays into the dining room or kitchen for coffee. But Chrisanne's presence made her feel self-conscious about wearing it. At the best of times, the peignoir was modest enough, but if she got hard…

Iris settled back in the lounge chair, forcing herself not to sit stiffly, and sipped her espresso.

"So…your dick," Chrisanne said slowly.

Iris sealed her mouth around the sip of espresso so she wouldn't spit all over herself. "I do have one, yes. What about it?"

"How does that even work? You fuck women? You look like a woman—."

"I *am* a woman," Iris said sharply, and swallowed her irritation of Chrisanne's thoughtless words. She'd had this conversation with too many people before, people who equated genitalia with gender, and attraction to that particular genitalia a determinant of sexual orientation. "I am a woman," she said again.

"But you date women who love pussy, most who'd rather not have a naked dick near them, unless they bought and paid for it." She seemed to be putting herself in that category. A woman who didn't want a real dick, or Iris, anywhere near her. At least not in *that* way.

"I don't force myself on women. I tell them I'm different from most women they've slept with and they have the choice to either sleep with me or not." She curled her lip. "It's not like my dick is this giant thing I go around slapping women in the face with, metaphorically or otherwise."

Iris thought she might have gone too far but Chrisanne giggled. "That would be so gross." Was she still drunk? She was silent for a few minutes. "So..." She bit her lip, looking curious and mischievous at the same time. "Can I see?"

Absofuckinglutely not. "I'm not a curiosity."

Chrisanne frowned. "You were okay with me feeling it last night."

"That was different, that was sex. This is you wanting to look at me like some circus freak. I'm not into that."

Chrisanne shrugged. "Fine." But she kept eyeing the hem of Iris' nightgown, her gaze considering, as if she hadn't felt her dick earlier that morning. Iris finally grunted in annoyance and went back to her room.

After stripping off the peignoir and robe, she fell back into bed, naked. She sent a mental "fuck you" to Chrisanne for interrupting her morning ritual and rolled over. She'd left the curtains open and sunlight fell over her bare limbs. For the first time since being at the villa, she lay in her bed completely nude. It felt good, free in a way she hadn't realized she'd missed.

Despite the sips of espresso, Iris easily fell asleep. And woke again in the early afternoon from a dream, Chrisanne crawling up the bed toward her, watching the slow and inexorable hardening of her dick, with her lips parted and ready to taste.

Iris trembled to full wakefulness, her hips fucking languorously into the bed. She pressed a hand between her legs and thought, with sleep fogging the edges of her awareness, of taking care of it there in the bed, stroking herself to a sweet release. But the thought of sleeping in the stained sheets later that night made her shudder with revulsion. She got up for a cold shower and more clothes than she'd had on in the morning.

In the dining room, the last of the buffet style lunch lay in warming trays, the crumbs on the table telling her that the other women had come and gone. Iris poured herself a glass of tomato juice and wandered out to the terrace where she and Chrisanne had had their morning conversation. She was surprised to have the terrace to herself, but her solitude didn't last long.

"I was wondering where you were."

Aisha and a pair of bridesmaids came out to the terrace looking sun-warmed and happy.

"I'm here." Iris spread her arms wide and tried for a smile.

"Late night?" Her friend sat down while the bridesmaids took out their iPhones and took selfies and pictures of the view, occasionally giggling at whatever they saw on their cell phone screens. They seemed to be deliberately giving Iris and Aisha some privacy.

"Something like that. Too much wine and not enough sleep." She didn't explain why but the smirk on Aisha's face said she didn't need to.

"Chrisanne was up early this morning. She went out on the yacht with our neighbor."

"Neighbor?"

"Yeah. Remember? The guy who plays guitar at all hours of the day and night. I think he's an insomniac or something."

Ah. "So she won't be going with us tonight?"

It would be the last night the bridal party would have to itself before the groom and his groomsmen arrived from Capri. The men had a similar set-up at a villa on the island and were slated to arrive by car the next morning. Everything seemed very complicated and lavish. And Aisha was very much enjoying her new rich lifestyle. Iris was just happy her friend loved her sugar daddy so much. It was convenient to be trapped in a wealthy lifestyle when your jailer adored you, and vice versa.

"No," Aisha answered Iris' question about Chrisanne. "She'll be back. She made a point to say we shouldn't leave without her."

"Okay then. I guess we won't."

"Do you want to leave her?" Aisha asked. "I thought you two were finally getting along well. After that blow up at the beach, didn't you just finally fuck the anger away and are now BFF's?"

"Come on, Aisha. You know I'm not into casual sex." Never mind that was exactly what would've happened last night if Chrisanne had been all the way on board. Iris breathed a quiet sigh. "We came close," she admitted.

"The extras?" Aisha asked.

"Exactly."

"I thought you told her."

"Why should I? I wasn't planning on sleeping with her."

Even the bridesmaids, who were pretending not to listen, laughed at that. "Girl, sometimes you are just so oblivious," one of them said. "It's almost cute."

Aisha plucked the tomato juice out of Iris' hand and drank half of it in one go. "Come on. Let's get you some aspirin and coffee so you can come with us to the shops. Maybe you'll find a nice dress for tonight."

After a shot of espresso and some Tylenol, Iris left the villa with Aisha and the bridesmaids. The girls were easy to hang out with, and the day went quickly with barely enough time for Iris to think about Chrisanne and the night they spent together.

They all bought slutty dresses for the night's party, ate pizza on the steps of the Amalfi Cathedral, gorged themselves on gelato, and chatted mindlessly about the wedding and plans for when they left the fairy tale weekend behind. Obviously, though, Aisha's fairy tale would continue with her prince charming and their new life. For Iris, it was back to Atlanta and the job she knew and the ruins of her relationship with Jasmyn. A cheering thought. The church bells tolled the third hour while they sat in the hot sun, their quartet a quiet ship in the storm of tourist activity.

"If I don't stop eating like this, I won't fit into my wedding dress." Aisha groaned and dropped back onto her elbows on the stone steps.

"I think you'll be fine," Iris said. "I'm the one who needs to worry about fitting back into my old life when I leave this place behind."

The bridesmaids hummed sympathy over their gelatos, their eyes hidden behind dark glasses.

"You got used to living like this in three days?" Aisha asked, laughing.

"What can I tell you?" Iris shrugged. "I get spoiled fast."

They soon left for the villa where they began the intricate process of getting ready for the night's outing.

Chrisanne made it back from her private yacht party in time to go out to the club with Iris and the other women. But Iris didn't talk with her, only gave her a brief smile while she regretted with every facet of her being the red wine that had led to this. At least she only had three more days of this to go. One night of partying with the girls, the wedding day, then the last day before they all scattered again to their separate parts of the world.

At the club, Chrisanne was chatty and vivacious in high heels and a clinging pale blue dress. Her mood was on ten. And it was obvious she was avoiding Iris. Iris tried not to get her feelings hurt, but they went ahead and did what they wanted anyway.

The bridal party was roped off safely in the VIP section, gazing out at the dancing crowd while Chrisanne chatted earnestly with Aisha. That was when Iris saw the girl. She was gorgeous. Just the type Chrisanne would attract. Fashionably dressed in a slim-fitting suit with her narrow eyes, and a soft-looking mouth that looked perfect for eating pussy. The girl kept staring at their group, eyes wandering noticeably to Chrisanne. Of course.

Aisha bought the table a round of shots to get the mood started, then once those shots disappeared, everyone else at the table started a round robin of drink buying until the group of women, except Iris, was mostly drunk, mostly talking shit, and mostly sprawled in the big leather seats watching everybody else dance. That was when Chrisanne plopped down next to Iris. She leaned into Iris' space, smelling of limoncello and expensive perfume.

"Listen," she whisper-shouted over the loud music. "About this morning…"

Her words fell away, like she hadn't planned on saying anything beyond that, maybe hoping that Iris would pick up the slack. But Iris didn't have enough experience with this kind of thing to help Chrisanne negotiate the landmines of her own desires. All she could do was back off when the woman told her no. That, she knew all about. It wasn't a new thing and she liked to think she wasn't desperate enough to chase when they both didn't want the same thing.

Iris raised her eyebrows and waited for her to go on, but Chrisanne didn't say anything else, just bit her bright red lips and looked down at the small space between them. Iris didn't take pity on her. That wasn't her job and Chrisanne had made it plain there was nothing for them to really talk about. They weren't trying to kill each other with meanness anymore. Aisha's wedding weekend would go on without them getting at each other's throats. They just wouldn't be friends – or lovers – at the end of it. No big deal.

Eventually, Chrisanne sighed and looked up, away from Iris and to the other side of the club. Iris wanted to give herself a mental high five (or get sad drunk) when Chrisanne saw the suited Italian woman and did a double take. *That must be it for our friendly talk,* Iris thought as Chrisanne straightened her dress and shoved out her breasts. It wasn't long before Chrisanne and the Italian woman started eye-fucking each other across the room.

"I'm going to dance." Iris put down her drink and got to her feet.

"What?" Chrisanne grabbed her hand. "Come on, we were talking." Chrisanne tried to grab Iris' wrist but she sidestepped the clumsy grip and went off to the dance floor that was being bombarded by an Auto Tune song she barely found tolerable. But it was better than enduring the pre-mating call of the Italian douche bag. Not that she knew the woman but she just seemed the type. Maybe it was her Versace tie clip.

Iris gave them what she thought was enough time to seal the deal, half-heartedly shaking her ass to three rounds of Euro trash pop before limping back to their VIP section, her feet throbbing in the high heels she shouldn't have worn. A couple of the bridesmaids were back, sipping fresh cocktails and talking with their heads bent together, trying to hear each other over the loud music. Unfortunately, Tie Clip had migrated closer.

Iris sank into the padded booth on the other side of Chrisanne. Her old drink, which had already been a little watery when she left, was gone. Just as she opened her mouth to ask where it went, a waitress appeared at the table with a fresh bottle of vodka and a carafe of orange juice. Ice clinked into her new glass. Chrisanne took the vodka and mixer from the waitress and poured her up.

"I was starting to wonder if you'd ever come back," Chrisanne said.

"I'm surprised you're still here." Iris knew from personal experience that Chrisanne was certainly open to the occasional one night stand.

"Where am I gonna go?"

Iris pointedly looked over her shoulder at Tie Clip who was back with her own friends, a mixed gender group, who looked like they were having fun despite having to get their own drinks and stand up in the crowded club all night.

"Oh, please. I don't mind a little club flirting but I'm hanging with you all this weekend. Aisha is more important than some random piece of ass. Fine ass, but still." Her eyes flickered briefly over to Tie Clip.

Iris didn't know what to say. She suddenly had more respect for Chrisanne than before, caught off guard by the girl's loyalty. Maybe *she* was the one who needed to check herself.

61

"All right," Iris said. "Cool."

She was about to say something else when Tie Clip made another appearance. "Hey, wanna dance?" the Italian woman asked.

"Sure." Chrisanne gave a little wave to Iris then stood up.

She stumbled off with Tie Clip to the dance floor, leaving Iris with the other bridesmaids who all looked up as one to give Chrisanne a united side-eye.

"I have no idea why she's even here," one of them said, repeating the sentiment of the weekend.

The others nodded in agreement while Iris watched Chrisanne.

She danced all over Tie Clip with abandon, grinding up on her and laughing, tossing her hair with a carelessness that looked completely genuine. If she hadn't made that statement about where her loyalty lay, Iris wouldn't have had any expectations. But when it came time for everyone to leave and Chrisanne was nowhere to be found, Iris was disappointed.

After three strippers, uncounted drinks, and an embarrassing mid-lap dance proposition, 4 a.m. came and went. Chrisanne was still lost in the club somewhere and the party showed no signs of slowing down. But Aisha's groom-to-be was due to arrive in a few hours, and the wedding was that afternoon. Aisha looked tired and the bridesmaids all looked drunk out of their minds. None of them seemed in any shape to hang out any more.

"You all can go ahead and leave," Iris said. "I'll wait for Chrisanne."

"No way," Aisha said. "We all came together and we're leaving together."

They split up to look for Chrisanne, agreeing to meet at the bar in twenty minutes, whether or not they found her. Iris had never been to that bar before but was familiar enough with the layout of bars the world over to search every place she thought of, even the back office. No luck. Twenty minutes later she was back at the bar with everyone.

"Any sight of her?"

Everyone gave their version of "no," and the bridesmaids all leaned in on each other, their faces saying they were completely done with Chrisanne. Even Aisha, the only one among them with the patience of a saint, looked annoyed. But she didn't give up. "Let's look again one more time, girls."

Iris, who had been ignoring her bladder for the last twenty minutes, dashed to the bathroom to relieve herself before going back to the search. Inside the women's room, the line was long, and the floor was a wreck of discarded paper towels and pieces of damp toilet paper. A little disgusting but she'd seen worse.

Instead of waiting, she shoved into the men's room across the hall. Unlike most lesbian bars Iris had been to, the men's room was just about empty. Of the three stalls, two of them were unoccupied. She slipped into one and pulled down her underwear with a quiet sigh of relief.

With the toilet seat pressing into her thighs through the layers of tissue paper, she dropped her head back. Where the hell was Chrisanne? They had all walked together to the club when it was light outside and would probably need to hire a car to take them back to the villa. Her pee splashed into the toilet. She thought she heard a noise, a shushing, a familiar liquid sound. Kissing.

She shook her head. Bathrooms were the same the world over, you never knew when you'd stumble into sex on your way to changing your tampon. She finished up and flushed, adjusted her underwear around her hips, the dress along her thighs and ass. Then a familiar sound made her pause. A laugh and a moan that brought back memories of the night before.

No damn way.

Iris left the stall and washed her hands, taking her time with the soap and hot water while listening for any other noises from the still closed bathroom stall. No other sounds came. But she gave in to an impulse and dropped down to look under the bathroom door. The sight of a familiar pair of high heels spread wide over polished Italian loafers made her jaw clench. Iris stood up and smoothed down her skirt, grabbed a handful of napkins to pull the bathroom door open.

"Chrisanne, if you're in there, we're getting ready to leave. Aisha's been looking for you for a while now."

She yanked open the door before she got any response from the couple in the stall. Seriously, this was Chrisanne's compromise for not going home with someone? Iris breathed through the fire blast of jealousy that stopped her in her tracks. You just dodged a bullet, she tried to tell herself. But *herself* wasn't buying it.

At the bar, she found a just-vacated stool and raised her hand to order a shot of peach flavored vodka. But changed her mind at the last minute and got a mineral water instead. She texted Aisha that she'd found Chrisanne and was just putting the glass of water to her lips when she sensed an attentive presence behind her.

"That was a little embarrassing."

She counted to five before turning to look at Chrisanne. She looked damp and overheated, like she'd been dancing. Or getting fingered in a dirty bathroom stall.

"Sorry I couldn't wait until you were done," Iris said, not sorry at all. "Aisha is ready to go. She and the others are still looking for you."

Tie Clip stepped around Chrisanne and into Iris' line of sight. "What is it, are you jealous?" the Italian woman sneered.

Iris curled her lip. She didn't look at Tie Clip. "Maybe you should text Aisha to let her know you're at the bar and you're ready to go too."

For a moment, Iris thought there was a flush of guilt to Chrisanne's face, a look of chagrin. Then Chrisanne crossed her arms. "I didn't know we had a curfew."

"Don't be an inconsiderate bitch. Just text Aisha so we can all go."

"Don't think I don't see the way you look at her." Tie Clip spoke up again, this time getting into Iris' personal space. "But she doesn't want you. How could she want someone deformed like you, a chick with a dick?"

Iris froze. She felt like someone had just thrown a drink in her face, ice cubes and all. "Excuse me?" But it was Chrisanne she looked at. Chrisanne avoided her eyes and grabbed the Italian woman's arm, hissed something to her that Iris couldn't hear. Tie Clip ignored her.

"She wants somebody normal." Tie Clip sneered. "That's why she is with me." She turned to Chrisanne. "Right, baby?"

"Oh shit, please stop." Chrisanne had the decency to look embarrassed. "Just stop!"

But the Italian woman seemed bent on doing the opposite. She drew back from Chrisanne's grasp and shouted something in Italian, raising her voice even more to say something about a "boy-girl." Iris felt frozen to the floor. Embarrassment and anger simultaneously burned her face and froze her hands.

Iris narrowed her eyes at Chrisanne. "Really? This is what you're doing?"

Chrisanne grabbed Tie Clip's arm, babbling apologies, and tried to drag her away.

But Iris didn't want to hear anymore. "I'll see you back at the villa," she said. She sent another text to Aisha and stood up.

But Chrisanne jerked away from Tie Clip who was still shouting in Italian to anyone who would listen. People looked her way, and looked at Iris and Chrisanne. Malicious laughter cracked from a corner of the club.

"No," Chrisanne said. "I think it's time we all left." She slipped her arm around Iris' waist, or at least tried to, but Iris pulled away.

"It's okay," Iris said. "Stay until Aisha comes. I'll get a taxi."

She turned away to weave through the club and the barrage of eyes watching her every step. But once outside the club and in the relative coolness of the night, she couldn't stand still. The night was too lively. The laughter around her too loud. She slipped off her high heels and began the short walk back to the villa. She didn't want to be confined in a car right now.

Iris couldn't believe Chrisanne had talked about her to a stranger, a stranger who humiliated her in public. It wasn't that Iris was embarrassed about people knowing she was different from what they expected. Hell, she wasn't ashamed of being herself. It was the fact that Chrisanne was so damn easy about a casual betrayal.

It was one thing if she didn't want to sleep with Iris; she wasn't the first and wouldn't be the last to turn her down for sex. But it was another to blab about what they'd done. Had she described everything she saw and felt with Iris to the Italian stranger? Anger bubbled out suddenly from the well Iris kept hidden.

"Fuck you!"

She shouted it to nothing. To the night air. To her own stupidity in trying to sleep with the woman in the first place.

"Iris!"

67

Beneath the harsh sound of her own breathing, she heard someone calling her name from what seemed like a long way off. When she turned it was Aisha. On the quiet side road, Iris could just make out the ghostly paleness of the bridesmaids' dresses, hear the solemnly slow click of their heels on the pavement. Iris continued walking, but slowed down enough for her friend to catch up with her.

"Hey." It actually hurt to talk, like she'd been screaming.

Aisha came close but did not touch her. "How are you holding up?" She'd gotten Iris' concise but thorough text about what happened at the bar.

"I'm holding. Nothing like this is going to knock me down."

"I hope not." Aisha bit her lip. "So, she told this stranger all about...?"

"Yes. I was an idiot."

"It's not idiotic to want affection, Iris."

"Is that what the kids are calling it these days?" She tried to inject some humor into her voice but had a feeling she failed.

"Fuck…" Aisha looked over her shoulder at the women behind her. "Do you want to talk about this?"

"Not really." It was actually the last thing she wanted to do.

"Okay."

The bridesmaids walked behind them, talking quietly, weaving into each other as they struggle-walked in their high heels over the cobblestones. The sight almost made

Iris smile. They were on a narrow side street, steep and dark, that could barely fit a SMART car. The women took up the entire street, walking fanned out like a peacock's tail.

Iris turned back to Aisha who now also had her shoes in one hand, walking thoughtfully by her side and not pressing her to talk.

Iris appreciated her silence.

The flash of car headlights from behind her jerked her from her silent introspection. The bridesmaids moved out of the way, flowing back to the edge of the road, still talking among themselves while the small car slowly passed them. Iris stepped aside with Aisha to allow the car its already narrow passage up the street. But the car stopped when it was abreast of them and the door opened, the car light flaring on to show the driver, small and curious-eyed, reaching back to take money from the passenger. Chrisanne.

When Iris saw who it was, she froze. But Aisha didn't have any such problem. She stepped the barely two feet toward the open car door.

"I don't think it's good for you to be here right now." She looked up the street then back to Chrisanne. "Just take the car the rest of the way to the villa. We'll be there soon."

Chrisanne stood with one foot outside the car, a hand braced on the open window. Iris didn't avoid her gaze but she didn't go out of her way to meet it either. The driver said something impatient sounding in Italian and Aisha leaned down to reply.

They were less than half a mile from the villa. An uphill walk which made the prospect of taking the car more than mildly appealing. But Iris would rather walk. Aisha rapped her hand around the edge of the driver's window.

"*Scuzami.*" She lifted her voice so the bridesmaids could hear her. "Do you all want to go in the taxi with Chrisanne? You might want to jump in there since you're wearing heels."

But the bridesmaids' refusal came one by one, leaving Chrisanne half-way in the car with her hand propped on the door and a hurt look on her face.

You don't get to feel that way right now, Iris thought, but she didn't say it.

"Okay." Aisha took charge. "Get back in the car, Chrisanne. We'll see you at the house." Without waiting for the other woman's agreement, she started to close the car door. Chrisanne yelped and yanked her foot back into the car just in time to prevent it from being slammed in the door.

"*Grazie.*" Aisha tapped the window again and waved the driver off. The interior of the cab darkened with the shutting of the door then the car was gone, wheezing its way up the road.

"That chick is some piece of work," Iris heard one of the bridesmaids say.

With her shoes still in hand, she continued walking up the hill in the wake of the taxi cab. It wasn't long before the taxi's lights disappeared around the bend and they were left with the sounds of their quiet footsteps.

"How did I even end up in this mess?"

"Because you like getting head." Aisha smirked.

Iris nodded, her mouth curving up without humor. "True."

Aisha slipped her arm around Iris' waist. She smelled of the bar, and of the last stripper's strong cologne.

"I think Marco will let me fuck him on our wedding night," she said out of the blue.

Iris nodded, re-routing her thoughts. Pegging was something she and Aisha had talked about before, speculating whether or not Marco would let Aisha have him like that.

"After all this time, you haven't done that yet?" Iris made her way carefully over the ancient street, bare feet tentative over the stones.

"Nope. I'll be taking his butt virginity on our wedding night." Aisha grinned. "It's one of the things I'm really looking forward to."

Iris made the effort to smile though she wasn't sure Aisha could see. "I'm sure he'll enjoy it."

Aisha pressed into her side. "You're the one who told me to try it with him."

"That was a million years ago." Or two.

"It's not every straight man you can go up to and say, 'honey can I fuck your ass tonight?' I had to ease the conversation on him."

This time real amusement made Iris laugh. Aisha's idea of easing someone into anything was to stuff their face with a favorite food then baldy ask for what she wanted while they were chewing. That had led to at least one incident of Iris breaking out her rusty Heimlich skills. "I'm sure Marco knew what he was getting into when he signed up to do the forever thing with you."

A smile brightened Aisha's face. "I think he does. He really accepts everything about me. I'm lucky I found him."

Iris felt a twinge of jealousy. With Jasmyn, she'd never felt that absolute certainty about their relationship. Even though Jasmyn had been the one who chased Iris and won her over, in their happiest moments Iris had only felt tolerated. The adoration she'd shown, her girlfriend treated like a burden, making Iris feel ashamed for loving so deeply. Then Jasmyn pushed her away until that love turned to ashes. But this conversation wasn't about her.

"Yes, you are lucky. It doesn't happen for everyone."

That last slipped out, but she couldn't catch it back.

Aisha's smile dimmed. "I know, honey."

Iris consciously relaxed. Tomorrow, she promised herself. Tomorrow, she would be a better maid of honor and not think so selfishly about herself. She sighed into Aisha's embrace and they walked the rest of the way back to the villa in silence.

The lights were on in the living room, but it was obvious that the two servants who stayed on the property were already asleep. Maybe Chrisanne had left the light on for them. Aisha pushed open the door to the main terrace and drew in a deep breath.

"You want to talk?" She gestured to the full bar that was stocked with both their favorites.

But it was obvious Aisha was tired. It had been a long night and she was getting married in the afternoon.

"No. I'm good. Go to sleep." Iris drew her into a hug, smiling when Aisha sagged into her in relief at having permission to go to bed. "We'll talk tomorrow. Or later."

"Yes." Aisha yawned, covering her mouth with the back of her hand.

"See you in the morning," Iris said. "The stylists will be here by eleven, don't forget."

"As if I could." Aisha made a noise, a pre-hangover wail. "Whose idea was it to have the bachelorette party the night before the wedding again?"

"Yours." Iris smiled.

"Ugh." Aisha's bedroom door closed on her groan of protest.

In her room, Iris showered away the smells of the bar and crawled into bed. But sleep didn't come. An hour later, she was still awake and thinking.

"Don't promise me forever if you don't mean it."

Iris remembered saying those words to Jasmyn, wanting to believe that, no matter what, they would stay together. But forever was a shorter time than even she thought. Barely two years, apparently. Sometimes she tried to look back and see what she'd done, or not done. Didn't she let Jasmyn fuck her enough? Was her constant cooking of Jamaican food what had driven her girlfriend to ask for, then demand, an open relationship? She knew it was stupid to even think about. Jasmyn's decision to want other people, then eventually *not* want Iris at all, had nothing to do with her. Right?

But why was she even thinking about that now? Jasmyn was half a world away in Atlanta.

Chrisanne.

Chrisanne was the reason. Iris sighed, annoyed at herself for coming so slowly around to the cause of her maudlin nostalgia. Chrisanne had just wanted a night of sweaty, nearly anonymous sex. And Iris would have been happy to give it to her; and had been more than ready to, before the usually slumbering worm between her legs got all into its feelings and decided it wanted to join the action.

Shit. When did she begin to think of her dick as a separate thing? Iris rolled over in the bed and checked her phone's clock again for the fourth time that hour. The numbers hadn't moved very far. It was still dark outside and she still had to be awake and ready to be a maid of honor in the afternoon for Aisha.

This wedding wasn't doing her any favors. If it hadn't been for Aisha's wedding, she wouldn't have met Chrisanne and she wouldn't be torn to pieces about a broken promise—Chrisanne's—that hadn't really been a promise at all.

The previous night came back to her in crystalline detail. Chrisanne's mouth heading steadily south, her hands tugging down the zipper of Iris' dress. Liquid bliss, then Chrisanne under her skirt, touching her, then jumping back as if bitten by a snake. Iris rolled her eyes at the thought.

Your dick again.

But…but wasn't it always about her dick? Wasn't the failure of that entire evening, the humiliation of this night, to be fully blamed on her fucking dick? Well, not fucking, as it turned out. There had been no promises on Chrisanne's part to keep what they'd done a secret but Iris had at least expected common respect from her. Common respect to privacy. Shit. Having expectations of strangers. Yeah, that was smart.

Annoyed again with the direction of her own thoughts, Iris left the bed in a rustle of sheets, pulled a thin robe over her naked body and moved toward the bedroom door. Maybe it was just time to get this out in the air with Chrisanne so she could get some damn sleep.

Iris gripped the door handle and pulled it open, gasped and almost fell into Chrisanne.

"Shit!"

It was Chrisanne who cursed. Iris stilled in the doorway of her bedroom, still surprised at Chrisanne's presence. She stepped back and took in the rumpled woman in her doorway. Bare feet. Wrinkled dress. Hair that looked like she'd been rolling around in bed for the last hour.

"What do you want?"

"I feel like I'm always apologizing to you," Chrisanne said.

"Maybe you should stop doing dumb shit."

Chrisanne flinched, but Iris refused to feel bad. Despite her earlier intention to find Chrisanne, she realized now that she wasn't ready to talk with her. She gripped

Chrisanne's arms and pushed her outside the doorway. "Seriously, you should leave."

"I already left you alone. That was the coward's way." She swiped a hand across her face, looking guilty and very, very sober. Unlike the moment they had confronted each other at the bar. "I'm really sorry, Iris. I say stupid shit when I'm drunk. I know that." She chewed on her lower lip. "It's not an excuse, believe me, but…"

"I'm sure you didn't say anything to that woman you didn't plan to. Obviously, you trusted her enough to rub all over your pussy in a dirty club bathroom." Iris crossed her arms.

Why was she even talking to Chrisanne? The girl had said everything she needed to say in the club. She'd done everything that Iris had ever needed her to do. She typically didn't like her partying with a side of humiliation but when she got it served to her like that, she could take a hint.

"I was drunk. I didn't know what I was doing. I…" Chrisanne took a deep breath and started chewing her lip again, so hard this time that Iris wouldn't have been surprised to see it bleed. "I didn't mean to hurt you."

"What you intended to do and what you did are two different things." Iris shook her head, suddenly impatient with the unproductive conversation. "I accept your apology. You can go to bed now with a clear conscience."

"Fuck. I wish it was that easy." But Chrisanne backed up in the doorway, her eyes downcast, her mouth red and ravaged. "I'll…I'll see you tomorrow."

"Yes. You will." Iris closed the door in her face and leaned back against it with a quiet sigh. She blinked into the darkness of her room, realizing that the tightness in her chest had eased just a little. She looked over her shoulder as if she could see through the door to where Chrisanne had been standing.

Huh.

But the situation didn't bear pondering, as she'd been telling herself all night. With a mental shrug, she got rid of her robe and climbed back into bed. She closed her eyes and was asleep in minutes.

Chapter 7

The morning of the wedding came much too soon for Iris. Bright sunlight broke into her room and woke her from an uneasy sleep. Barely four hours. And—she grasped for her cell phone to look at the clock—just a half an hour before the makeup artists were due to arrive and get everyone ready for the wedding.

The villa was flooded with people from eleven o' clock on. First with the arrival of the stylists, then with the rush of the women getting themselves ready for the quiet arrival of the three o' clock wedding at the nearby church.

Women with over-sized suitcases skittered down the hallways, disappearing into the bride's bedroom before coming to find Iris and the bridesmaids. Chrisanne wasn't in the wedding party, but her presence in the house was unavoidable. Once, Iris noticed Aisha pulling her into a secluded corner. The next time she saw Chrisanne, she looked like her pet turtle had been run over. Twice.

Iris barely had time to think about what Aisha said to Chrisanne before it was time for the men to arrive, the groom, his groomsmen, and the best man rolling into the village in their black cars just in time for the ceremony.

Marco, big and handsome, and his tribe of men he'd known since college and before, all came sweeping into the church glowing with health from their version of the pampering the women had been indulging in for the past few days.

The church was beautiful, and the ceremony relatively quick, leaving everyone misty-eyed or at least gritting their teeth with jealousy. Aisha had found her super-rich Prince Charming and was getting ready to spend her honeymoon soaking up sunshine on a yacht floating across the Mediterranean. Who wouldn't be envious of that?

Just for Aisha, it was a perfect day. A light sprinkling of rain at the beginning of the afternoon for luck and afterward, brilliant sunshine. Watching the new bride and groom dance in the middle of the ballroom, it was easy for Iris to believe in love, and in happily-ever-afters.

"They look good together, right?" Chrisanne came out of nowhere to stand beside Iris.

"They do," Iris said. She sipped her champagne and waited for Chrisanne to move on.

She'd been in her head for most of the day. Thinking again about Jasmyn and the promises they'd made to each other in their two years together, about what her life in Atlanta was like, if she would be changed after seeing one of her oldest friends manifest the love she'd always wanted. Too much thinking, in other words.

But Chrisanne didn't go anywhere. If anything, she made herself even more comfortable next to Iris, only disappearing briefly to get a drink before settling in on her cocked hip. Finally, Iris couldn't take it anymore.

"What do you want, Chrisanne?"

The ice in Chrisanne's glass rattled when she sipped her drink. "I thought we were good?"

Iris didn't hide her surprise. "What made you think that?"

"You said you forgave me last night." She actually looked offended that what she'd assumed wasn't true.

"I probably said that it doesn't matter. That's not the same thing as forgiving."

"Then if it doesn't matter, why don't you just forgive me now and get it over with?"

"Maybe because you're an entitled bitch?"

"Ouch." The ice cubes rattled again and Chrisanne didn't say anything for a while. But her silence was too good to last. "When I went out with the neighbor last night, he told me I was making a big deal out of nothing."

"So, you talked to some other anonymous person about what went on in my bed." Iris wanted to slap her.

But Chrisanne grabbed her arm, the coldness of the glass transferred to her fingers and sinking into Iris' skin. "It's not like that, and I didn't tell him anything. I wasn't drunk yet."

"Is that supposed to make me feel better?" Iris could feel the anger bubbling up in her throat along with the urge to shout at Chrisanne. Around the room, no one was paying attention to them. She didn't want that to change.

Iris leaned in, hissing. "Why don't you just fuck off back to the States and stop trying to stir up bullshit?" It wasn't a suggestion. "I don't want any of what you have to give, and I think it's tacky of you to try this at Aisha's wedding when you claim to be such a good friend."

Chrisanne flinched back from her with a sharp cry. "I *am* her friend," she said.

More than a few heads turned in their direction but Iris put her back to the room and tried for a smile.

"You want to take this someplace less public?" she asked.

She wanted to be finished with the conversation all together but Chrisanne seemed bent on having it. Iris didn't wait for her but walked away from the dancing and happy laughter, determined not to ruin Aisha's day. She thought she saw Aisha glance toward them over her new husband's shoulder but she wasn't sure.

She wove through the crowd of guests, nearly fifty people enjoying the sunlight and happiness around them, and ended up on one of the rear balconies. The shadows of dusk had already claimed the back of the house, the sun falling quickly and leaving the balcony and the garden below it shadowed in gloom. It felt right to take Chrisanne into the darkness and away from the sparkling happiness of Aisha and her new husband.

Iris didn't wait to go on the attack. "If you're her friend, why are you here? The bridesmaids all hate you." *And I kind of do, too.*

Chrisanne crossed her arms over her chest, the hand with the drink balanced on the opposite elbow. "Hate me? Or do they all want to be me?"

Her cocky grin sent a spike of anger straight to Iris' fists. She stepped back and gave Chrisanne plenty of room. "Why do I even try with you?"

"Because…because—" The over-confidence fell off Chrisanne's face like an ill-fitting mask. "I'm sorry. Shit." She gripped her elbows tighter and looked away, the tendons in her neck tight. "Sometimes I just can't help myself."

"No kidding."

"Listen!" Chrisanne looked back at Iris. "I'm asking your forgiveness. Just like you asked Aisha to forgive you years ago. It may not seem likely to you but this isn't something I normally do. I'm just…" She gestured to Iris' body. "…this is all new to me. You've had your whole life to deal."

Iris sidestepped her mention of Aisha. What she and Chrisanne had brewing between them was different. "This is not about you having a meltdown about almost fucking someone with a real dick. That I get. I've been having this same conversation with potential lovers my whole adult life. Some say no way, some say yes. That's fine. What's not fine is you telling some random bitch about my life. That's the very opposite of what you do when you say you like someone."

Chrisanne looked stricken, face tight, eyes narrow. "Fuck. I'm sorry. I'm sorry."

"Stop apologizing!" She didn't mean to snap, she really didn't. Iris backed away from Chrisanne even more. The girl was turning her into something she didn't appreciate. "Your empty words mean nothing." Iris took a deep breath to let out the truth. "And that's okay."

"That's *not* okay though." Chrisanne's voice rose sharply. "I want—"

She broke off and darted across the space separating them. Her mouth crashed into Iris' just as her drink spilled down the lemon yellow of the maid of honor dress. Ice skittered across the floor. Iris jumped back, hissing at the cold liquid soaking into her chest through the dress.

"What are you doing?!" Iris tugged at the wet material over her breasts.

Chrisanne looked both miserable and excited. "Let's finish what we started the other night." She fumbled with the now empty glass and kicked at the ice cubes skating across the painted tile floor.

Iris remembered vividly that Chrisanne hadn't gotten the chance to finish with the Italian woman last night. All that pent-up lust.

"Are you that desperate for a fuck?" she asked. "Go back to that Italian bitch if you're so hot to get off."

"Don't insult me, and don't insult yourself, Iris. You know it's not her I really want. Can we just rewind and pretend last night never happened?"

"You're asking a lot."

"No, I'm not." Chrisanne lapsed into silence, but not for long. "I saw how you were watching Aisha and Marco."

Iris opened her mouth to deny it but Chrisanne cut her off. "I was looking at them the same way."

Chrisanne sighed, a sound of loneliness that touched a chord inside her. Maybe the only difference between her and Chrisanne was that she wasn't trying to fill that empty space inside herself with the temporary affection of strangers. At least not Italian ones.

Chrisanne cupped Iris' elbows, gentle and tentative, like approaching a wild horse, and slowly drew her close. Iris allowed it. They kissed.

Maybe they weren't that different after all. Warm bodies. Wet lips. Sighs that leaked into the midsummer night like prayers to an indifferent god. The cool and damp spot on her dress became warm, pressed between her body and Chrisanne's.

You need to stop.

This is stupid.

Don't be so desperate.

All these thoughts came and went while Iris tasted the gin on Chrisanne's lips. The tartness of lemon, the wet lance of mutual lust.

"Let's find a bed," Chrisanne muttered into her mouth, squeezing her waist. "I want to see you."

A hot ache settled low in Iris' belly. "We should—" She hissed when Chrisanne stroked her nipple through the dress. "—we should let Aisha…know we're leaving."

Chrisanne squeeze her nipple, a sweet and rhythmic distraction that made her nether lips itch with the first trickles of wetness. "I'm sure she'll figure it out."

Iris pulled away from Chrisanne's mouth. "I'd rather let her know myself."

They left the balcony and found Aisha sitting on her husband's lap and laughing, surrounded mostly by people Iris didn't know. She whispered in her ear that she and

Chrisanne were leaving together. Aisha grabbed her hand with a question in her eyes.

Iris nodded and Aisha let go, but not before directing a hard look at Chrisanne.

They left the ballroom to the interested and amused eyes of the bridesmaids and a few of the groomsmen, walking quickly side-by-side and not touching until they were shut away inside Chrisanne's room, the balcony doors shut, both their eyes open.

Iris wanted to be careful, to go slow and give Chrisanne the chance to change her mind, but Chrisanne didn't allow that. Without a word, she stripped. The peach-colored dress, bra, and panties tossed aside, the full-hipped body pushing Iris backwards toward the bed before she could get a good look. The backs of Iris' knees hit the bed. She breathed quickly, her mouth dry. She twisted her arm back to unzip her dress.

"No," Chrisanne said. "Let me." She licked her lips. "Turn around."

Behind Iris, she knelt on the bed. The sound of the zipper being undone was slow and unbearably arousing in the quiet room. Chrisanne's fingertips trailed down the skin she slowly revealed, and Iris shivered from the contact, equal parts nervousness and desire.

She was so lost in the sensation that she almost missed the sound of Chrisanne's quickly indrawn breath when the dress fell to pool at her feet.

"I swear, you're the most gorgeous woman I've ever seen."

Hands touched her back then low on her hips where her garter belt rested. Iris yelped in surprise when teeth nipped her ass. She spun around. "Hey!"

"You look so good. I had to have a taste." Chrisanne grinned, then her eyes dropped to Iris' crotch. She sobered and Iris swallowed.

"Get on the bed," Chrisanne said, her voice gravely and rough.

Iris climbed into the bed, nearly falling over in her haste to spread herself out for Chrisanne. She lay there, bra and stockings and garters and panties on. Between her thighs she was slippery and overheated, her skin quivering with arousal.

"I'm going to take these off now," Chrisanne said.

"Okay."

It felt like she was being visually devoured, savored, stockings rolled slowly down with her foot resting on Chrisanne's shoulder, Chrisanne's eyes on every aspect of what she was doing, missing nothing of the skin she uncovered. When she pulled the tight fitting panties off, a slow and deliberate peeling away of layers, Iris sobbed with relief.

She was so wet. So hard. Her dick very rarely perked up when she was with a lover, but with Chrisanne...

Christ!

Every inch of her was ready for pleasure. She groaned, eyes squeezed tightly shut as Chrisanne leaned over her, sliding up, incidentally brushing her breasts over her dick and stomach, to unhook her bra. Iris sighed as the fabric, white lace she'd brought just to wear under her maid of honor dress, released her breasts. Her nipples were hard and aching to be touched. Chrisanne sat back. She was thorough as she looked at Iris, the both of them sober, everything between them out in the open.

Chrisanne licked her lips. "Do you want to fuck me?"

Jesus...

Iris' hips bucked in answer. "Whatever you want," she gasped, nearly desperate for it. "Just as long as you touch me."

She tried not to notice the way Chrisanne skimmed over her dick, the barely half palm-full of balls, to the dripping urgency of her pussy beneath, her eyes taking in the whole package, so to speak, though she did not touch. Chrisanne came close enough to make Iris groan from the sweet heat of her so very near, then she straddled her hips, her mound a careful distance from Iris' leaking dick.

She wanted so much that it *hurt*.

"You're beautiful," she said. But she didn't look at anything below Iris' heaving belly.

She flushed with a kind of shame she hadn't felt in a long time, fumbled to lever herself up on her elbows, to try to leave the bed, but Chrisanne pushed her firmly back down with a hand between her breasts.

"You're beautiful," she said again, like she was trying to convince herself, because she still didn't do more than glance quickly at Iris' dick.

Iris was used to this, but it still hurt. That pain didn't disappear with Chrisanne's slow stroking of her breasts, her thumbs and forefingers plucking at Iris' nipples until she arched off the bed, whimpering her pleasure.

"I'm going to fuck you tonight," Chrisanne said. "Just tell me that's okay."

"Yes." Iris licked her dry lips, trying to catch her breath. "Please fuck me."

Then Chrisanne slowly sank down until her wet pussy, surrounded by its immaculately shaved bush, pressed down onto Iris' dick, pushing the weeping head flat against her belly. Iris threw her head back and shuddered to the very depths of her soul.

Chapter 8

Iris woke up to silence. The near inaudible hum of the party being over, the drinks done, and every one of the guests gone home. Chrisanne lay beside her, turned away in sleep, lips parted and moonlight spilled over her bare shoulders and back.

Iris blinked away the last of sleep and slipped silently from the bed to pull on her wrinkled maid of honor dress. The door clicked quietly open under her hand. At the end of the hallway, a soft light glowed. She followed it to find Aisha, loose-limbed and relaxed on the couch, her hair a wild mess around her face. She was eating a chocolate croissant.

"It was that good, huh?" Iris smiled at her friend.

Aisha loved to eat chocolate after really good sex. Said it kept the orgasm high longer and was better than any cuddling or pillow talk.

Aisha nodded, smiling with her eyelids low. "I could ask you the same thing."

Iris sat down in the couch, stretching out her toes to nudge lightly at her friend's. "I enjoyed everything about tonight, we both did."

Aisha smirked. "Everything?"

Iris flushed at the memory of Chrisanne's slick pussy lips pressing her dick flat and sliding along its length like a curious amusement park ride. That beginning had shocked Iris' body into an intense spasm of pleasure, making her go off like a rocket in the first thirty seconds of them fucking.

But after…after Chrisanne had made it last, her fingers fucking into Iris with thorough and deep stokes that rolled her hips in the sheets and had her begging for more.

"Damn, I didn't mean to take you back there." But Aisha was smiling, wide and amused. She licked a smear of Nutella from the corner of her mouth. "But it was good?"

"It was everything I expected to get from someone like her."

Aisha nodded as if she understood perfectly. "What are you going to do?"

"Nothing I wasn't going to before. Head back to Atlanta and my real life. The only fairy tale to continue is yours, honey." She smiled to soften any sting that might be in her words. Just because the fairy tale romance and courtship hadn't been hers didn't mean she wasn't happy that one of her best homegirls found it.

Aisha hummed a sort of response and nudged the platter with two more croissants on it in Iris' direction.

Iris took one. "Thanks."

The croissant was buttery and warm still, like she'd heated it in the oven instead of the microwave, real heat that lasted and wound through the bread, making the surface slightly crisped and flaky and the chocolate hazelnut filling burst out, warm and gooey, onto Iris' tongue. She moaned in not-so-silent appreciation.

"Damn," Iris said. "Where did you find these things?"

"I'm not going to tell you. You'll have to visit me again to get more."

Iris slowly chewed the buttery croissant, savoring the dark sweetness of the Nutella on her tongue. "That sounds strangely fair."

"So seriously. What's up?" Aisha glanced down the hall, as if expecting Chrisanne to burst into their quiet nest any moment. "Is this just a foreign fuck or are you trying to make something out of this? I don't want anyone to get hurt," Aisha said. "Especially not you."

Iris swallowed for a moment, the last bite of the croissant stuck in her throat. This was the woman she'd been shitty to for years just because she valued Aisha's identity as a lesbian over her value as a friend. She'd thrown away years of friendship just because her friend found she liked dick in addition to the pussy she'd loved to eat since they were in college. As if what Aisha chose to put in her mouth was any damn business of hers. And here Aisha was being worried about Iris' stupid hurt feelings.

"I'm fine, Aisha." She curled in the couch toward her friend. "I'm not taking this too seriously. I'm sure tonight was just an apology fuck for her. Under normal circumstances, this chick wouldn't have given me the time of day, and I know that."

"Would you have given her any play in Atlanta?" Aisha asked.

"No."

Iris was more into harder women. Ones who liked button-down shirts and preferred to do the fucking. But because they'd been trapped together for each to get more than surface impressions of the other, Iris had fallen for

Chrisanne's raw humor, her sense of style, the way she didn't give a shit about what anyone irrelevant thought about her. It was a bonus that she was Jamaican too. But none of that mattered.

"I'm heading out soon," Iris said. "I doubt I'll see her again."

"Are you sure that's the right thing to do?" Aisha frowned.

"I wouldn't say right, but that's all I have now."

She didn't say anything about the low thrumming in her veins when Chrisanne touched her, the winged riot in her stomach when, just a few minutes before, she'd paused getting up from the bed and watched Chrisanne's sleeping and resisted the urge to slide back into bed with her and cuddle until the sun came up.

These were foolish feelings that would disappear once she got back to her real life. Right?

"Don't you think you should talk at least once, while you're both sober, about the shit you all did when you were drunk?"

Iris deliberately side-stepped the question. "I thought only lesbians were supposed to be fans of processing and 'unpacking' emotions." She made air quotes with her Nutella-smeared fingers.

"We bisexuals can do that shit too." Aisha ate the last of her croissant and licked the chocolate from her fingers. "It's good policy to know where you stand with someone you slept with."

"I know where Chrisanne and I stand. Separately. This is a vacation fuck. We both go our separate ways with some interesting memories to take back to our real lives. Done."

Aisha rolled her eyes then got to her feet. "You're a damn mess, girl." She drew Iris into a Nutella scented hug. "I'm going back to bed. If you're gone by the time I get back, I'll understand. Just take care of yourself."

"I always do."

"I wish that was true." Aisha's smile was bittersweet. "When I come back to the States for the sociology conference next year, I'll make sure to pass through Atlanta and see you."

"Good." Iris squeezed her tight, trying to make her friend understand everything in that simple touch. This was the last time they would see each other for a while. "I want only the best for you."

"I love you, too." Aisha chuckled. She understood.

They shared a smile, both sweet and sharp. "Be happy, honey," Iris said. "You deserve it."

"I could say the same thing to you."

They drew apart and looked at each other. Then Aisha swatted Iris on the butt and walked back down the hall, her hips swaying as she tossed a smile over her shoulder. "Try to get another round in before you go. From what I heard last night, you won't get pussy that good again for a long while."

Then she was gone, disappeared into her bedroom with her new husband, leaving Iris with burning cheeks and the thought of actually waking up Chrisanne for one last goodbye "kiss."

But in the end, she didn't wake Chrisanne up. Instead, she went back to her own room to shower and pack before getting in her rental car for the long drive back to the airport in Naples. The drive gave her plenty of space to think. By the time she was on the plane, she'd managed to convince herself that the past few days had meant nothing more than seeing an old friend again, and incidentally getting off with a forgettable stranger. It was a nice illusion.

Chapter 9

After Iris got back to Atlanta and back to the office, it seemed like everybody had wedding fever. One of the lawyers immediately demanded wedding pictures from Italy, said she was planning something incredible for her and her partner of ten years now that they could finally be married, while the baby dyke who temped for them whenever the main office receptionist was out, gushed about her girlfriend of three weeks and thought she was great "wifey material."

Iris humored them with smiles and the requested pictures, but at the end of her long first week back, she was ready to ram wedding invitations down everyone's throats. They all seemed so happy and oblivious to the heartbreaks waiting for them around the nearest corner, while Iris had front row seats to one of her own.

On Sunday, five days ago, she'd come in from the airport to see her half-empty condo and a note from Jasmyn saying she'd moved out and was taking everything she bought with her. Never mind that they'd gone half on most of the furniture. Iris wanted to curse and demand Jasmyn bring her stuff back. But she only dropped her bags in the corner of the room before falling into bed and staying there until it was time to get up for work on Monday morning. The exhaustion stayed with her until the relief of Friday rolled around. Then she ran out of the office as quickly as she could, leaving all that talk of weddings and faithful love behind.

At home, Iris dropped her purse on the built-in bookshelf by the door, grateful that the shelf was part of the house otherwise Jasmyn would have taken it too. If she lost any more furniture, she'd be living in a bare box. Only the bed remained in the bedroom, her clothes moved to shelves in the closet for Jasmyn to make off with the antique dresser they'd both found at a thrift store while on vacation in Savannah.

Iris' keys clanked in the glass bowl and she kicked off her heels and made her way toward the kitchen for a glass of iced water. The summer was already a boiler.

She leaned against the counter, drinking from a clear highball glass with only the sound of her slow gulps in the air-conditioned room. That sound almost drowned out the stomping up the hardwood stairs just outside her still open front door.

Jasmyn walked in. Sweaty and butch-looking in cut-off shorts and a tank top that bared her muscled arms and showed off the meaty handful of breasts that had initially drawn Iris like a pig to mud. She closed her eyes on a sigh. Maybe it wasn't healthy to compare herself to a pig.

"Do you even care that I'm leaving you?"

She opened her eyes to see that Jasmyn, stubbornly asshole-ish with a fat hickey on her neck, had come closer, trudging into the condo with her shoes on. Iris had walked past her and her U-Haul on the way into the building, but hadn't noticed the hickey at the time. Classy.

She put the nearly empty glass on the counter.

"Would it matter if I cared?" Iris asked.

This conversation was just a formality. She wondered why Jasmyn even waited so long to get her things out of the apartment. She could've taken everything while Iris was gone.

"You say you're leaving," Iris said. "There's nothing I can do. I'm not begging you to stay."

"So you were lying when you said you want us to work."

"Working on a relationship takes two, Jaz. And you're already gone."

Jasmyn had been gone for months. She'd simply taken the coward's way out and waited until Iris was gone to the other side of the ocean to tell her what was really up. Polyamory was what she wanted, but Iris wasn't one of the many lovers she wanted to lavish her attentions on. It was unfair as fuck, but she wasn't going to humiliate herself any more by begging for something she was never going to get. If it was one thing she learned from Chrisanne, it was the futility of banging her head against a stone. That was what crying for love from Jasmyn amounted to.

"Because of that simple reason, we're way past begging," Iris said.

"I'm not so sure." Jasmyn put her hands on her hips, legs spread in that cocky way Iris had always loved. "Why don't you try now and see?"

Iris laughed. She couldn't help it. This was such a bunch of bullshit. One last moment of humiliation before Jasmyn left her to live with her commune of fuckable girls who waited at her leisure for food and sex. She pushed herself away from the counter and turned around with a suck of her teeth.

"Get the rest of what you want," Iris said. "It'll be dark soon. You wouldn't want to fall down the stairs with my bookcase on your back."

She finished the last of her water, and almost choked when Jasmyn's hand closed on her shoulder. She froze and swallowed thickly. Then was surprised when she didn't get that feeling of weightlessness in her belly, weakness that meant she was breaths away from giving in. She noted the absence with wonder.

Iris turned. "What?"

Jasmyn's hand fell away. "I should be asking you that? What the hell happened to you in Italy? Did you get some new ass at the wedding? Is that why you're acting brand new?"

She said it like it was the least likely of scenarios. Like Iris couldn't get someone to fuck her if her life depended on it.

But Iris couldn't just spit out the truth of what happened with Chrisanne. It seemed so crass to admit that she had eaten someone else's pussy in Italy, that someone else had had their hand on her dick and didn't run screaming from the room. Well, at least not the second time. But her hesitation told the important part of the story.

"For real?" Jasmyn's eyes widened. "Was it some used up Italian hooker who dropped to her knees for a few Euros and sucked your limp dick?"

"Seriously? That's how you're talking to me now?"

This had always been a sore point between them. Iris' dick. It didn't matter that Jasmyn had been the one who pursued Iris with the full knowledge of what lay between her legs. A hidden part of Iris knew that Jasmyn always considered her a challenge, a trophy she'd won. The ultimate femme who didn't need a strap-on when it came to getting down. But Iris didn't always get hard. Jasmyn hated that and considered it a personal insult.

Before Jasmyn could respond, Iris' cell phone chimed from her purse. She grabbed it on the fourth ring.

"Is she there?"

Her brother's voice on the other end made her sag a little in relief. "Yes. Why, what's up?"

"I'm coming to get you. Leave her there to get whatever she wants."

Ian had her spare key, too. She'd asked him to look in on the condo while she was away, just in case. He must have seen the slow emptying of it and known what Jasmyn was doing.

She stepped away from Jasmyn who'd followed her from the kitchen, and padded barefoot to the far window of the nearly empty living room. "How did you know?"

"Don't worry about that. I'll be there in about three minutes."

She wanted to tell her brother that things were cool and she didn't need his rescue. But Ian often knew these things before she did, just like she sometimes knew his aches before he was aware of them.

"Okay." She hung up.

Iris took a breath and circled back through the living room, past Jasmyn who followed her like a ghost, and grabbed her purse.

"I'm heading back out." She went to the mat by the front door where she'd left her shoes, slid the high heels back on. "Get everything you want tonight." Just then, she decided to change the locks in the morning, even if she had to get up at a ridiculous hour to get it done.

"Where are you going now? You just got here."

"That's none of your business, remember? You're moving out. You don't want to be part of my life anymore." And Iris realized she didn't want Jasmyn in her life either. It just took her a long time to finally admit it. "Lock up behind you. I'll see you later."

She left the apartment and clattered down the stairs just in time to see her brother pull into the parking lot, his low slung cream Porsche the most expensive thing there. His window slid down, showing his mock scowling face. Ian winked.

It was impossible to miss that they were twins. Their faces, angular with matching dimples and perfectly symmetrical lips, were nearly identical. Ian was often called pretty, while Iris, who though she got the better end of the deal, was simply referred to as striking.

"Get your ass in here, girl."

The passenger door popped open and she got in.

The car smelled like Ian's expensive cologne. Something that was pheromone-based and probably sold for hundred of dollars an ounce. It smelled nice of course, but Iris wasn't going to tell him that.

"What are you doing in this part of town?" She buckled her seat belt as he put the car back in gear. Her brother lived in Buckhead and worked there too.

"She's cleaning you out, but I bet she waited until you got back in town so you could see it and be all torn up about how she found someone else so fast."

Iris didn't deny the truth. Over the years, she'd been oblivious to Jasmyn's ploys, but Ian saw through them like cheap glass. He always told her Jasmyn was only into her for the novelty of it. She'd never wanted to believe that. If she didn't think twice about what was between her legs, then why would Jasmyn, someone who hadn't freaked out when Iris told her, find it such a big deal?

"When I got home from work she was already there," Iris said. "Most of the stuff in the apartment is already gone. I don't know what else she can take."

Her brother didn't say anything but the engine growled like it was an extension of him, pissed off at Jasmyn enough to bullet through a yellow light.

"I'm glad she's gone," he said. Then he looked away from the road to glance at Iris. "She *is* gone, right?"

"Yeah..." She sighed.

She was as done with Jasmyn as Jasmyn was done with her. There was nothing left between them except the last few pieces of furniture her ex still coveted. She could have whatever the hell she wanted. They were just things. As long as Iris had her bed, it was cool.

That Sleep Number bed had cost a small fortune. Or a fortune for someone who made the kind of money she did. Enough to keep her in vintage dresses and classic perfumes but not enough to spend five grand on a bed and shrug it off. That had been a significant portion of her savings. She still hadn't built her savings account back up to what it had been before.

"I need you to sound more confident than that," Ian said.

But Iris only shrugged. She was doing her best. And it really wasn't that she had any lingering feelings for Jasmyn. All those had been crushed in Italy. Between listening to Aisha talk about what real love was supposed to be, drowning her sorrows in the wetness between Chrisanne's thighs, and just letting the Italian sun burn away her worries, she was damn near a new woman. A new Jasmyn-free woman.

They drove a few more miles in comfortable silence, the purring quiet of the car's engine, no music but the quiet reflection of their thoughts.

"Here's the place."

Ian pulled the car into the parking lot of a bar Iris had passed a few times but never ventured in. The valet greeted Ian by name and Iris rolled her eyes at her brother. He grinned, passed the young man his keys, and cocked out his elbow for Iris to take.

"I can walk my own damn self in, thank you."

But he didn't take the elbow back, if anything he stuck it out even more. "What are you, five?" She huffed and hooked her arm through his.

"Five-year-olds don't drive Porsches," he said.

Iris rolled her eyes. The car was a relatively new purchase, a present to himself when he made partner at his midtown law firm. A justifiable expense, he'd said. After all, an entertainment lawyer with clients like his couldn't drive to important meetings in a decade old Nissan.

Inside the bar was one of the most festive happy hours Iris had ever seen. A live band covered Neo Soul hits, background to ringing laughter and loud conversation from nearly every corner of the place. A group of men shouted Ian's name and gestured him over.

They looked like his type, successful almost forty-year olds with the look of money, new and old. They were all attractive in that Atlanta hetero way that Iris had come to recognize over the years. Well-groomed, tight bodies, discreet designer everything, and an air that said they were the cream of the man crop in any room they walked into. More than half the time they were right since most of the women who seemed even vaguely interest in men were openly admiring them. Ian's arrival brought a fresh wave of feminine interest and a few discreet masculine stares.

She greeted her brother's two best friends, Cedric and Percival ("call me Al"), and slipped into the empty chair at their table. They knew she was into women but that didn't stop them from the harmless flirting they'd fallen into the habit of doing over the years.

"You're looking sexy tonight, Iris." The youngest one of the group, Cedric, gave her the usual once over. "Are you sure you and this fool are related?"

"Unfortunately, yes." She flashed him a smile. "I have the childhood trauma to prove it."

"Buy her a drink and quit your foolishness, Cedric." The most laid back of them, Michael, gave Iris a one-armed hug after greeting her brother with a hand clasp and chest bump. "Welcome back from Italy," he said. "You want us to get you a San Pellegrino or some shit?"

"You can keep that," she said. "Give me a single malt, light on the ice."

Cedric whistled. "My kind of girl." After he asked the other two men what they wanted, he left the table to get the drinks.

It didn't take Iris long to fall into the familiar rhythm of hanging with her brother and his friends. She didn't do it often, but when she did, it was fun. They didn't hold back around her, figuring as a lesbian, she was an honorable brother anyway. They pulled her into their flirtations with other women, talked shit, bought her drink after drink until she forgot about what was happening in her condo, damn near forgot her own name toward the end of the night. Hours later, they were all decently drunk, although Iris was getting hungry. When she leaned over to share this with her brother, he nodded.

"The food here is shit," Ian said. "Even at half price, it's not worth it."

Michael swayed closer, his swagger loosened by at least four drinks. "Let's take the party to that Italian joint next door. The food is good and the waitresses are hot."

That was enough of an endorsement for Iris. They ended up at a table at the back of the busy restaurant. Drunken elbows on the table, irrelevant conversation batting between them while a too-cold A/C blasted over their shoulders. She shivered in her light cotton blouse and rubbed her palms over her bare arms. Cedric immediately shed his blazer and handed it to her while Michael arched his eyebrow. "You know you'll never get any pussy off her, man."

"I think she made that pretty clear years ago, Mike." Her brother said it the same time Cedric growled. "Damn, can't this just mean I'm being nice?"

"No!" They all chorused, even Iris.

They laughed just as the server came up to their table. Iris discreetly checked her out. Michael was right, the servers there were gorgeous. Her subtlety got blown out of the water when the girl met her eyes with a flirtatious purse of her lips and a smile. Her brother chuckled. Iris blushed and tried to look innocent.

She glanced away from the curvaceous YaYa DaCosta look-alike and caught a flash of a familiar figure across the restaurant. Long legs, muscled thighs and a high ass packed tight in a black skirt. She drew a breath of surprise, but when she got the courage to look higher than the woman's ass, she disappeared behind an incoming party of six. She frowned. Were her eyes playing tricks on her?

"And what would you like to eat, ma'am?"

The server's provocative voice pulled Iris' gaze back to her. "I bet I know what you'd like to eat." Michael's whispered comment made her kick at him under the table.

But it was Cedric who jumped. "Damn! I didn't say shit."

The server smiled even more and stepped closer to Iris. "You can have anything you want tonight," she said. "Anything."

Along with sobriety, subtlety was also apparently dead for the night. Iris swallowed and looked down at her menu for the first time that night. She could go where the pretty server was leading. She was just the type that Iris liked, leanly muscled with a pretty face and a boyish edge. The restaurant's tuxedo uniform suited her to perfection and her soft lips, red and moist in the intimate lights of the restaurant, looked very kissable.

But Iris couldn't get that brief glimpse of the familiar body out of her mind. It couldn't have been her. It really couldn't. She'd left Chrisanne a world away. What happened in Italy had nothing to do with what was happening now, or what could happen with the server tonight. But Iris' mind was no longer in the game. She may be drunk but instead of wanting to suck on the server's pretty pink mouth, she was thinking about going home to bed and reminiscing about her week in Italy. She cleared her throat, and purposely did not look at the server.

"I'll have the dinner portion caprese salad. That's all."

She only looked up after the server left the table, her manner obviously cooler after Iris' dismissal. Michael took a large sip of his new drink. "If that girl spits in our food, I'm blaming you."

Cedric laughed and looked across the table at Ian. "I bet you'd never turn down pussy like that. She practically threw it on your face."

Her brother shrugged. "It looked free, but I'm sure Iris would have paid for it one way or another." He looked at Iris in question but didn't say anything about the server. At least not yet. He'd get to her about that when they were alone. She sighed and reached for her water. It was time to start sobering up.

By the time Ian was sober enough to drive her home and Iris was drunk enough to let him, it was well past three in the morning. She stumbled into the condo, ready to collapse in her bed without even brushing her teeth, bypassing the light switches to make her way in the dark to her bedroom. Iris threw her purse toward the bed and started to strip off her clothes. Then froze at the heavy thud, the sound of her purse hitting the rug instead of the soft bed.

What the fuck?

She fumbled for the light and stared, open-mouthed, at what she found. Or didn't find. The bitch Jasmyn had taken her bed too.

Chapter 10

At work the next Monday morning, the wedding fever continued. A smiling co-worker, Janice from contracts, dropped an envelope on Iris' desk while she was making the final arrangements for her boss's business trip to Seattle. It looked suspiciously like a wedding invitation.

"I hope you can come." The girl, who looked far too young to be marrying anyone, gave a sighing smile. Her look was earnest and sweet.

Iris, sucker that she was, smiled right back and continued typing. "Of course, I will. Congratulations."

Janice leaned down to give Iris a quick peck on the cheek then walked off, grinning broadly. Iris kept typing, kept smiling although it felt more like a grimace. Oh, wedding season…

She considered it a personal victory when she didn't snap an hour before the end of the day when another envelope dropped on top of a stack of reports she was organizing. She didn't look at the envelope but narrowed her gaze up at the latest interloper.

"When are you getting married?" she asked.

Marina, the receptionist who recently celebrated her eleventh wedding anniversary, stared at Iris like she'd lost her mind.

Iris shook her head. "Sorry. I didn't realize it was you."

"You might need to take a break, you've been staring at those files too long if you're already hallucinating." Marina flicked the envelope with a chubby finger. "This is for you.

111

It's from a vase of flowers waiting for you out in reception."

Iris frowned at the envelope. It was square and note-sized, too small to be a wedding invite. "Why would you bring me this and not the flowers too?"

"I didn't want to get in your business."

Iris stared at Marina until the older woman squirmed and shifted from foot to foot. When she decided she'd been enough of a bitch, she stood up. It had been a long day of working practically non-stop; she felt a little cranky and a lot cross-eyed. Iris picked up the envelope but didn't open it.

"Since you don't want to get in my business, can you tell me what the envelope said?"

"It's sealed." Marina looked disappointed. "I couldn't read it."

Iris laughed wryly. "Let's go, nosy."

At the receptionist's desk, a tall vase of flowers took over nearly half of the space. The arrangement was all tropical and wild, nothing generic about it with its bright ginger blooms, curling twigs, and sensual orchids. It was very impressive.

"Damn, that's nice." Whoever picked the flowers had great taste.

"Thanks. I chose them myself."

Iris stopped before touching one of the bright ginger stalks. She turned slowly, frowning, because this *couldn't* be who she thought it was. But the woman who unfolded herself from one of the leather couches in the reception area was indeed Chrisanne. She was casually dressed in a tank top, jeans, and high heels. A light blazer was draped over one arm.

"Chrisanne."

"Say it like you missed me," she said, smiling.

Iris was very aware of both Marina and the receptionist watching them. She tried very hard not to stare at Chrisanne and her unfamiliar casual beauty, but she didn't think she did a very good job if Chrisanne's creamed cat smile was anything to go by.

"What are you doing here?" Iris asked.

"Coming by to invite you to dinner."

"I'm at work."

"Well, I hope you'll leave here sometime today and grab a bite with me." Chrisanne's smile turned positively wicked. "However you'd like."

Behind her, Marina giggled.

Okay, this is getting ridiculous. "You should come back when I'm done here," Iris said.

"I plan to. Just wanted to give you a warning of my plans." Chrisanne took a card out of her purse and slid it into Iris' hand. "Here's my number. I'll be back here at about five fifteen. Call if you want me to come get you earlier or later."

Her over-confidence, as usual, rubbed Iris some kinda way. "What if I don't want you to come at all?"

"Not an option." Another wide smile.

It was nothing Iris hadn't expected her to say. "All right. I'll see you tonight at five thirty. But I want you to follow me home. I'm not leaving my car here."

"A woman who wants to get straight to it." Chrisanne grinned. "I always liked that about you."

Iris didn't dignify that with a reply. She only gave the flowers another brief glance before heading back to her desk.

Although she would never admit it to anyone, she was eager for the end of the day to come. Seeing Chrisanne in reception had fizzed unexpected happiness through her veins. Until that moment, she hadn't realized just how much she missed her. Sitting at her desk, Iris licked her lips and swore she tasted Chrisanne on her tongue. Effortlessly, she remembered the rasping moans that left Chrisanne's mouth when she came, and how she looked spread across the sheets, sated and satisfied.

Before she left her desk at five ten, exactly, she texted the number Chrisanne left and walked to reception, took the flowers from the now empty reception desk and placed them on her own before taking the elevator down to the parking garage.

So close to their meeting, she purposely didn't think about what could have brought the girl to Atlanta and to her office. She didn't think about the last time she'd seen her, stretched out in the bed they'd shared for a few hours, her body sketched in moonlight, her mouth pinked and swollen from their shared kisses, from the rasp of Iris' pubic hair and the other things they'd shared that night. She didn't think of any of these things. She didn't.

When she pulled her little blue Mazda out of the garage and met Chrisanne in her convertible, she led her through the side streets of Atlanta to the parking lot of her condo. In the shelter of her car, she took a deep breath before getting out and climbing into the sleek black Audi with Chrisanne.

The car smelled new. The black and burgundy leather was butter soft under her back and thighs. Iris pulled the car door shut and closed them into silence. Chrisanne was there. Beautiful and close, smelling like sweat and that citrus perfume that reminded Iris so strongly of Italy that her mouth watered.

"Do you want to have dinner here instead?" she asked.

A smile perched at the corners of Chrisanne's mouth. "Here, in the parking lot?"

"Don't be a smart ass."

But her facetious question gave Iris the space to think maybe having dinner at her place was a bad idea. Italy was the past, this was her real life. The two did not need to meet. But still, here, Chrisanne felt different. Before Iris could take back her invitation, Chrisanne shrugged.

"Sure. We should have dinner here. It would be nice to see the domestic side of you."

They sat in silence for a few heartbeats before Chrisanne parked the car properly and turned off the engine. Iris fumbled with the handle to get out and led the way to her second floor unit.

The place was as empty as Jasmyn had left it. And it seemed even more so now with someone else there. Iris clenched her teeth, determined not to apologize for her lack of furniture. At least there was food in the fridge.

Iris dropped her purse in its now customary place on the built-in bookshelf. "Make yourself comfortable."

"It's a little empty in here, isn't it? You redecorating?"

"You could say that. This is the minimalist my-ex-took-all-my-shit look."

Chrisanne smiled briefly. "I can't say I'm familiar with that but I can empathize."

Jasmyn took nearly everything that hadn't been nailed down. The only saving grace was that Iris didn't believe in knick knacks, so when Jasmyn took the coffee table and armoire, she hadn't left random shit just sitting on the floor. The living room was bare except for a thick rug that took up over half the floor, a gift from her mother when she came back from Turkey nearly twenty years ago.

Otherwise it was the closed French doors leading out to the patio, the built-in desk and bookshelves—Iris had been surprised Jasmyn didn't take the small chair she'd bought to go with the desk—and a couple of paintings she'd had before they moved in together. Even the dining room was an empty space where the dining table and chairs used to be, the chandelier hovering over nothing but the blank space where love and respect, perhaps even tenderness, had once lay.

Iris turned away from it all. "Is there anything you don't eat?"

Chrisanne turned away from her examination of the room. "I'll eat anything you put in front of me." The corners of her mouth twitched up, and even Iris had to smile.

She decided to make something quick for dinner. Between the pantry and the fridge, she already had the ingredients for most of her favorite ten-minute dishes. She wasn't in the mood to linger in the kitchen while Chrisanne examined her condo's empty spaces.

"The bathroom is down the hall if you need to use it," she said before she went into the kitchen.

She wasn't surprised when Chrisanne followed her, and was mostly silent while she put together the simple meal of caprese salad, warmed bread served with olive oil, and half a baked chicken she'd picked up the day before. She spread a picnic blanket under the chandelier and lay out their dinner with a pitcher of water and a bottle of chardonnay.

"It looks delicious," Chrisanne said, joining her on the floor.

She sat Indian style despite her tight jeans and immediately reached for the wine. Her hand around the long neck of the bottle quivered slightly as she poured the chilled chardonnay into her glass. Surprised, Iris looked into Chrisanne's face but saw no sign of nervousness. It was all in her hands, all in the wine she was all too eager to pour. So…she wasn't as confident as she seemed. And that made Iris finally begin to relax. She drew a silent breath.

"Tell me, what brought you to my office today?"

Chrisanne held the wine glass in her hands and took a quick sip, then two. "I live in Atlanta now," she said. "I got a job with Price Waterhouse Coopers."

That was not what Iris had been expecting. Seeing Chrisanne at the restaurant a few nights before, that she could pass off as a hallucination. But them living in the same city seemed like some huge cosmic joke. Would she have to avoid her like she planned on avoiding Jasmyn?

"I don't—" She began to speak but Chrisanne cut her off.

"Why did you leave?" Chrisanne looked up at her from under her lashes, mouth still dark from her lipstick, a smear of wine making it glisten.

For the first time, she sounded like the younger woman Iris always wanted to treat her as, her voice with a slight tremor, vulnerability in her smooth and unlined face. "I was ready for more," Chrisanne said. "For whatever you were ready to share with me. But you left."

Iris hissed at the pain she felt radiating from Chrisanne. She wiped her hands on her thighs and used that small amount of borrowed time to debate her choice of words. "I didn't think you wanted me. And I wanted you too much."

"But that's stupid." A flash of a smile took the sting from Chrisanne's words. "Why would you run when you could feel how good things were with us?"

"We were drunk half the time we fucked! How could I trust any feeling that came out of that?"

"We're not drunk now," Chrisanne said, and the words hung heavy with expectation.

Even as Iris breathed deeply at the possibilities between them, her thighs clenching at the images that bombarded her brain, she shook her head. "I don't want to complicate tonight with sex."

"Are you sure sex wouldn't just simplify things?" Chrisanne held the wine glass in both hands, taking occasional swallows but did not put it down.

"No. It wouldn't. You pulled yourself away from me after that first night. *After* sex. The kind of sex we can have scares you. How would me stripping down for you again and waiting for your rejection simplify anything?"

"I'm not going to reject you. I never did. You just caught me by surprise."

"If by *surprise* you mean blasting my business all over the Italian coast, then I guess, sure, you were surprised." Iris clenched her hands in her lap, caught off guard by how painful the memory was.

"I was stupid," Chrisanne said, dismissing that earlier version of herself with a pained look. "I was scared. Like you did when Aisha told you she was bisexual, I thought about what other people will think, not about what I want. Your dick is unexpected, but so are the feelings I have for you. It took a few days and a hard look at myself, but now I'm ready to embrace both those things." Chrisanne put down her wine glass and braced her palms flat on the floor at either side of her hips. "I want to fuck you again, and I want you to fuck me. But I also want more."

Iris was glad she didn't move. She wasn't sure what she would do. Could she believe what Chrisanne said? Not that it mattered, because she *wanted* to believe it. Weakness had already invaded her limbs and stolen her hunger for food. She'd made a beautiful meal but all she wanted was to sip the faint traces of wine from Chrisanne's lips and feel if her skin was still as soft as it looked. But after dealing with the aftershocks of her uneasy two years with Jasmyn, she was trying to be better about her life decisions. "Don't do this if you're not for real, Chrisanne. I can't go through this again with you."

"Do what? You're acting as if I forced you into bed with me, and forced you to enjoy it."

"I'm not saying that. Stop playing the martyr. You know we were only there together for fun. This is real life now. You have no obligation to find me and start this up again."

"You think I'm only here out of obligation?" Her gaze was hard, flint dark and direct.

Hurt and pride radiated from her like poison. Iris didn't want to hurt her feelings but she didn't want to get her own feelings hurt either. She didn't want to turn this into a *Waiting to Exhale* tragedy, bringing a vacation fuck home only to have it turn sour under the pressures of every day life. If that was really an option. Maybe Chrisanne just wanted to fuck since she didn't know anyone in Atlanta yet.

"Stop guessing my motives!" Chrisanne leaned into Iris' space. "Why don't you just ask me what I want? Or better yet, just listen."

This was such a different tone from the one Iris was used to that she froze, not knowing what to say. She cleared her throat.

"Then tell me what you want. Tell me why you're here and what you think having dinner with me will accomplish."

Now that she had the floor, Chrisanne seemed dumbstruck. She bit the corner of her lip and looked away from Iris, her gaze skittering over their dinner and the few feet of space between them. She sighed.

"I'm here because I like you. A lot," Chrisanne finally said. "And I want to make this work. It was hard for me to understand what I was getting into while we were in Italy, when you first showed me..." She trailed off.

"My dick." Iris knew she was being confrontational, but she also knew if they didn't get the difficult things out of the way, they would just end up wasting each other's time.

"Yes." Chrisanne actually looked away, color rising under her dark cheeks. "Yes, your dick." Her voice was stronger. "I haven't fucked a guy since high school, and even then I did it because I thought that's what I had to do."

"I'm not a guy—"

"I know, I know! Just let me say this before I puss out." She cleared her throat again. "You know how most Jamaican parents are. While the rest of the world was fighting for marriage equality, my parents still thought it was okay to stone the batty man who lived down the lane from us in Jamaica. I couldn't be who I was around them.

When I left high school, I left them and their small-mindedness behind. And I left dick behind too. Even though your dick isn't attached to a man, the fact that you have it still fucked with me." She bit her lip again, refusing to meet Iris' eyes. "But then...after you left me in Italy, I was so damn hurt. I was looking forward to waking up with you and exploring the coast together, maybe drive back to Naples and get to know each other separate from all the drama of the wedding.

When you left, I thought you were being doggish, like guys I'd fucked in high school who didn't give a shit once they got their nut." Finally, she looked up at Iris, her eyes wide and slightly wet. "But even when I thought that, I knew it couldn't be true. I still wanted to get to know you. Aisha said you were scared and didn't want to get hurt again, especially after what I did at the club." She blushed again and squirmed, shifting like there was no place on the picnic blanket she could get comfortable. "I was an idiot. I didn't think it through. Even though it's not an excuse, I was drunk. But I'm not drunk now and I want to explore a future with you if you can give me the chance."

Iris released her clenched teeth from the inside of her cheek, the only way she could be quiet while Chrisanne talked.

"I've been hurt badly in the past," she said. "I don't want to go through that again."

"I can't promise I won't hurt you. In case you haven't noticed, I'm a bit of an asshole." Chrisanne shrugged, looking sheepish. "But I want you in my life. You're from

Jamaica, too. You make me laugh. You don't give a shit how much money people make. You're happy with your life and you make me want to be better." She reached for Iris' hand. "Can't that be enough for now?"

Iris shook her head, but she already knew what her answer was. "Yes, it can. It is." She didn't need an excuse to step toward Chrisanne like the other woman was stepping toward her.

"Thank the Lord!" Chrisanne sagged where she sat, her face a mask of exaggerated relief. "I've been stalking you for days, hoping you'd turn up at what everyone says is the most authentic Italian place in the city."

Iris breathed through her own sense of relief and felt a loosening of the tightness in her chest. "You could've just asked Aisha for my number."

"I did. She wouldn't give it to me. But she told me what part of the city you live in, which actually helped a lot." A look of embarrassment flickered over Chrisanne's face. "My apartment isn't too far from here"

"So you're really stalking me?"

"Just a little. I didn't want to leave things unfinished between us." She grinned. "Besides, the sex was fucking amazing. Who can give that up?"

Iris shook her head, finding herself both charmed and a little scared by Chrisanne's youthful enthusiasm. She cleared her throat, not sure if this was the right time but wanting it with a sudden desperation that made her breathless. "Speaking of sex, do you want to um…?"

123

Chrisanne shot to her feet, nearly getting tangled in the picnic blanket. "Yes." She flushed again and helped Iris to her feet. "Let me help you put the food away first."

They made quick work of the food they didn't touch, stuffing all the containers into the fridge without properly re-wrapping them, including the wine. Iris hesitated at the kitchen sink with the nearly full bottle of wine in her hand, half aware that it wasn't going to be any good the next time she opened it. But that thought quickly washed away when Chrisanne put her hands on her waist and pushed her back into the counter until the tops of her ass pressed into the granite. The bottle thumped on the counter, but didn't spill.

"Show me your room."

It was her voice that did it. Low and urgent with heat, it made Iris' panties pull tight against her moistening flesh. But even though Chrisanne demanded to see her room, she pushed into Iris' hips with her own. Iris whimpered at the press of her stiffening dick between them. She blindly reached for Chrisanne and slotted their mouths together. Twin groans filled the kitchen.

"I missed the way you taste," she gasped into Chrisanne's mouth.

It was more the way she kissed, an all-in sensuous dance of tongue and lips, her mouth latching on to Iris' like there was no other sustenance she needed. A hot and sweet sucking on her tongue while her hands roamed over Iris' back and low on her hips, pressing them urgently together.

Chrisanne pulled back. "If you don't want me to get pussy juice all over your counter you need to show me to your room now."

But Chrisanne was already moving them back, guiding Iris toward where she guessed the bedroom was. Her guess was good enough, so Iris closed her eyes and enjoyed the feel of that hot mouth on hers, the firm pressure of Chrisanne's thumbs tilting up her jaw so she could nibble and suck her neck. Iris shivered. Then winced when her shoulder hit a doorway. Her eyes flew open.

Yes, the bedroom...this way.

She guided Chrisanne past the guest bathroom and to the bedroom. She scrabbled backward with her hand for the door handle, turned it, and pushed it open.

Chrisanne stopped dead. "Where is your bed?"

Fuck.

In the rush of all the blood in her body flooding south, she forgot about the lack of an actual bed in her bedroom. Since Jasmyn left and took her bed—she'd called to curse her out and demand it back—she'd been sleeping on a pile of comforters in the middle of room. But that didn't matter now.

"My ex." Iris squeezed Chrisanne's breasts through her tank top. "She took it."

"Fuck her then."

"No." She fumbled with the buttons of Chrisanne's jeans. "You fuck *me*."

"You're so corny." But she seemed very much on board with that plan, yanking down the zipper of Iris' dress and pulling it off to toss it carelessly aside. "Shit." Chrisanne stepped back. "I actually forgot how beautiful you were." She stared at Iris' body, on display in (thankfully) matching bra and panties.

Iris was soaking wet and desperate to get her mouth all over Chrisanne. She yanked down her own panties and got rid of her bra. "Stop telling me and show me."

"Fuck, you're bossy."

But luckily Chrisanne followed orders well.

Once they were in the pile of blankets on the floor, Iris took control. It had been so long since she'd been with a woman who wanted all of her. She quickly peeled off Chrisanne's clothes and pressed her down into the blankets, planting kisses over every inch of her she could reach.

Chrisanne smelled like that same perfume she wore in Italy, and of lemons and desire. Iris licked and bit her all over, making up for the days she'd been without. She inhaled her lover, pressed her nose into her small creases, sucked her fingers, drank the sweat from her skin.

And finally, finally, when she couldn't wait any longer, she lifted her mouth from Chrisanne's breasts.

"I want to taste you," she said. "Can I?"

Yes!" Chrisanne gasped. "God, yes."

Iris made her slow way down the writhing body, pausing to kiss and stroke the curve of her belly, her sharp hipbones, the silken skin on the inside of her thigh.

She felt so fucking good…

When they'd fucked in Italy, Iris thought the magic of that night had been due to the wedding and the sounds of the night, the violin, and the faint rush of the sea coming in through the windows. But she felt the same sense of wonder now, her entire self focused on Chrisanne's pleasure, her body burning with a need to satisfy even as her pussy was slick with arousal and her dick was hard enough to pound through steel. She pressed her hips into the blankets to relieve some of her own ache, an unconscious movement that she intensified once she realized she was doing it.

They both groaned at the first stroke of her tongue on Chrisanne's pussy. A deep and shuddering connection clicked between them.

"Jesus…I think you're trying to kill me." Chrisanne's hand dropped away from her head to clench in the blankets.

Her slick pussy lips were meaty and hot under Iris' tongue, sliding wet and humid, tasting of sex and everything good Iris had ever had. She pressed Chrisanne's thighs open even wider, reached up to stroke her nipples and twist them while her mouth devoured and sucked and licked. Iris pushed her hips into the blankets, fucking into the firmness under her while she fucked Chrisanne with her tongue.

"You're so good to me…" Chrisanne whispered, bucking up so hard that Iris had to brace an arm across her hips to hold her down.

With her mouth lavishing Chrisanne's clit, Iris stroked her entrance with light fingers. Her pussy opened up for her, slick and greedy. Iris licked the soft pink flesh to prepare her, then slid in two fingers, curled them up.

"Oh!" Chrisanne propped herself up on her elbow, staring at Iris. "More," she begged, her eyes heavy lidded, her mouth swollen. "Give me more."

Iris gave her another finger, stroking deep in her hot pussy, the slick sound of the fuck washing over her ears, grinding her hips into the sheets.

"Yes..." Chrisanne moaned and dropped back into the blankets. "You're so fucking perfect." She gasped again. "So perfect..."

She fucked Chrisanne deep and slow with three fingers until the muscles of her arm burned with the effort, until the sweat dripped down her face, and down the valley of her spine. God, she loved this. She loved how Chrisanne's face twisted, her look becoming desperate with each thrust of Iris' fingers and every flick of her tongue on her clit.

Even with her mouth full and her hands occupied, Iris kept her eyes on Chrisanne's face, wanting to see every play of lust there. There was so much beauty. So much—!

The muscles of Iris' pussy jerked tight.

"Fu—!" She grunted as an unexpected orgasm burned through her own body. The rhythm of her fingers stuttered but she kept going. Her eyes slammed shut and her hips bucked into the blankets the same time she felt a clenching around her fingers. Chrisanne stiffened all over and cried out.

"Fuck! Iris...Fuck..."

They shuddered together, pleasure rippling between their bodies in a feedback loop until Chrisanne collapsed into the sheets, laughing through the last of her orgasm.

"Glad I could make you happy." Iris panted.

Slowly, she pulled her fingers back from Chrisanne's pussy and flopped onto her back.

"I didn't doubt you would." Chrisanne whimpered and followed her across the sheets, draping her body on top of Iris', kissing her, breathing hard against her parted lips, her eyes still bright with a mixture of lust and satiation. Iris gladly swallowed her kisses.

"God! You're so. Damn. Amazing." Chrisanne punctuated each word with a kiss and reached down between Iris' legs.

Iris tore her mouth from Chrisanne's at the first touch of fingers on her dick, unhesitating, a squeeze and a slow stroke.

"Jesus…" Iris gasped.

Then Chrisanne's fingers went lower, teasing the opening of her pussy and loosening another moan from Iris.

"I want to make you feel good," Chrisanne murmured.

But she was already making Iris feel *fantastic*, decadent and wet with want, her entire body throbbing and tender in places that scared her. Her heart thumped with each stroke of Chrisanne's fingers. She slid into Iris like she was coming home, a sigh of pleasure as she teased her with delicate fingers, stroking under the tightness of her balls. It was just like last time, only better. This time, Chrisanne touched all of her, her dick, her tiny balls, her slit that dripped and begged for attention.

Chrisanne dipped her head lower, breath scorching Iris' stomach. Her muscles clenched in anticipation of the hot touch on her pussy, her throat hollowed to moan out her pleasure from the now familiar feel of Chrisanne's tongue lapping at her sensitive opening. But Iris cried out instead, a shout, when the hot mouth surrounded her dick.

"Fuck!" She panted. "What...?" But she lost all her words, breath stuttering with the uncertain heat around her. She held her hips still, unable to quite believe it. Chrisanne was—she was...

"Is this good?" Chrisanne lifted her head. "Sorry if I'm a little out of practice." She licked the head of Iris' dick, tongued the slit with a moan that hinted of surprised pleasure.

Iris quivered and gasped, her hands twisting in the sheets. Sweat beaded along Iris' spine. Her upper lip felt hot, too hot, and she couldn't catch her breath. Her thighs trembled and ached from where Chrisanne was holding them wide. "You're doing...fuck! You're doing great."

The last word ended in a gasping whine when Chrisanne licked the veined underside of her dick. She looked up at Iris through her lashes, eyes wide and innocent while her mouth locked tight around her cockhead. Chrisanne licked her again, her tongue circling, then she sucked with a hint of teeth that made Iris' breath catch and her heart threaten to punch its way out of her chest. Iris whimpered again, the heat gathering in her spine. She was about to come. So damn fast. She groaned in both arousal and disappointment. Then her mind grayed out completely as the orgasm slammed her down into the sheets, gasping.

"Oh fuck!" Chrisanne pulled off her dick, coughing as streaks of watery cum dripped from her mouth and down her chin. "Ugh!—this part I didn't miss." She wiped her mouth with the back of her hand. "Gross."

"I'm sorry," Iris gasped, her hips still bucking minutely into the empty space where Chrisanne's mouth had been. Her belly rippled with the aftershocks of her orgasm. Between her legs was wet and tingling, her pulse-beat strong there. "I'm sorry." It had been so long that she wanted to cry, and then she did, tears leaking from the corners of her tightly closed eyes. *Shit.*

"It's okay." Chrisanne followed Iris down into the sheets with her mouth, she tasted like cum and pleasure, a bitter white. She was smiling. "I want all of you," she said between kisses. "If this is part of it, then I want it too." Chrisanne kissed her again and Iris twined her legs around her, pulling her closer.

She swallowed past her panting breaths again, waiting out the slowing hurricane of her heart.

"So…" Chrisanne's smiling mouth teased hers. "Do you feel complicated now?"

"No, I don't feel complicated." Iris had to laugh at that. "I feel good." She licked her own slightly swollen lips, tasting the hint of musk from Chrisanne's pussy.

It felt decadent and right to lay in the aftermath of really good sex with Chrisanne, in her own bedroom. Everything in that room was hers, even if there wasn't much to it.

"What's on your busy mind?" Chrisanne moved against her. "I know it's something."

Iris smiled. "I was just thinking that I have everything I want right here in this room, right now."

Chrisanne pursed her lips, obviously thinking about just how many ways the answer was a deflection. Then she shrugged. She fluttered her fingertips down Iris' stomach, a light tickle in the sweat gathered there. Even in the low light, Iris could see the hesitation in her features now that the want between them was temporarily sated.

"I don't always know how to be a good person." Chrisanne's words were a soft and low murmur in the room. "But I want to be a good person for you, and for myself too. You're the first person that made me want to be different. I want you to know that."

Iris leaned up on her elbows to look at her. "I don't want you to change for me."

"No, you're misunderstanding me. I'm not saying you make me want to start pinching babies' cheeks and adopting abused animals or any crazy shit like that. I'm saying that I want to be nice to you, I want to help make you happy." She pressed her fingers lightly to Iris' lips. "Meaning I want to add to your happiness, not take away from it."

That was probably the sweetest thing anyone had ever said to Iris. She stroked her thumb across Chrisanne's lower lip.

"Okay," she said. "Whatever that looks like, I'm ready for it."

Chrisanne's features changed like lightning, a smile like the sun pushing away the gathering clouds. "Good." She jumped up to crouch over Iris, her teeth bright against the dusk of her face. "Now, I'm hungry. Feed me! I remember there was some chicken you were anxious for me to try."

"Right now?" All Iris wanted to do was roll over and sleep.

"Of course! Aren't you hungry too?"

"I just ate." Iris flicked a suggestive glance down to Chrisanne's bush.

"Woman cannot live by pussy alone, or dick." She cupped between Iris' legs, and Iris shuddered, still sensitive after her orgasms.

Chrisanne's gaze sharpened at the reaction. She stroked Iris again, watching her face the whole time.

"Fuck..." Iris breathed, her hips jerking into Chrisanne's touch, and away from it, like her dick couldn't decide what it wanted. "You need to stop." The too-soon stimulation hurt, but also felt good.

Chrisanne licked her lips, her glance dipping down to see what her fingers were doing. "You mean stop playing around and just fuck you already?"

"You're the one who wanted actual...oh...digestible food."

"I'm entitled to change my mind." Her fingers drifted lower, circling the sensitive opening to Iris' pussy, a light touch in the wet remnants of her orgasm. "I could fuck you all night." Then she drew her fingers away with obvious reluctance, licking them one by one.

Iris' stomach clenched hard at the sight. Her legs drifted open and she licked her own lips again as new arousal trickled down. Her dick twitched with interest but it was her pussy that was all-in this time. She opened her mouth to invite Chrisanne to taste her again, to flutter that sweet tongue where it had played and sucked before.

"Chris—"

"You know, you're right. We have time to do this again." She swirled her tongue around her two middle fingers. "I have years to find out what makes you scream my name." Her fingers left her mouth with a pop. "But my stomach is hungry right now." She smiled, all mischief. "Come on, gorgeous. If the chicken is as good as you say, I'll let you ride my strap while I play with your cute little titties."

Chrisanne was already fighting her way out of the blankets, naked and energetic in the light coming in from the balcony. It wasn't Italy, but the magic was similar, maybe even better. Iris smiled and allowed Chrisanne to tug her up from the sheets, all lightness and promise.

"I'm going to hold you to that," Iris said.

"Good." Chrisanne smiled and pulled her close. Her eyes shimmered with an emotion Iris had never seen in them before, something that glinted faintly of forever. "Kiss me," she said.

And Iris did.

"That Girl, She's a Killer"

A bored Louisa was a dangerous thing. She stood outside the bar smoking a clove cigarette and plotting her escape. Her best friend was off on her honeymoon while the second and third runners up bounced around the bar with their asses hanging out and attracting men Louisa wouldn't let lick her boots. If she heard one more comment from a stranger about the "ice water" in her veins, she would do something her friends would regret. Welcome to New York City on a Saturday night. Boring.

Normally, when the girls asked her to come to something like this, Louisa would tell them to go fuck themselves, in a nicer way of course, but she'd been in a stupidly generous mood after the wedding where her best friend finally got the man she deserved. Whoever heard of celebrating the bride when she was half way around the world probably riding her new husband to paradise and back.

Louisa really was getting too old for this bullshit. She took a deep drag from the cigarette, wincing at the smoke's burn through her lungs. A man sidled up to her with an unlit cigarette between his lips.

"Hey, gorgeous. Got a light?"

Yeah. Too old for this bullshit.

Louisa sneered at him, put the cigarette out under her stiletto and walked away toward the curb. She lifted her hand for a cab. She would text the girls and let them know she was heading home.

"Wait a minute, bitch."

Bitch? How original.

The man with his cigarette had somehow found a light but lost his manners in the process. She didn't look away from the street with its slow 3 a.m. traffic. It was cold. Her breath puffed clouds in the air from the fourteen-degree temperatures. Only the smokers had braved the outdoors, and right now it was just Louisa and Mr. Manners. That fact seemed to give him unnecessary confidence. He grabbed her hand and spun her to face him.

"I'm talking to you."

Louisa felt a tight jolt in her belly. Her pulse slowed down and her awareness of her surroundings sharpened. A nearly empty sidewalk. The lights of the surrounding high rises. The steady but anonymous whoosh of passing cars. She looked at the stranger who was a few drinks past good sense. He was attractive in that frat boy sort of way, if a girl liked that sort of thing.

"I *wasn't* talking to you," she said, keeping her voice low.

"You're so soft with them." A female voice, smoky and Australian-accented, reached Louisa from the nearby darkened alley. "Such a good girl."

Louisa sighed, wishing that it took her at least a few seconds to place that voice or even reconcile it with this very different place and situation from the last time she'd heard it. But no. She immediately knew who it was. And the heartbeat she'd slowed before began to speed back up.

Because this woman in this place could only mean one
thing.

Danger.

Louisa clenched her fist and tugged her hand back from
Mr. Manners, no longer in the mood to play. "It's been
fun," she said injecting a note of regret into her tone. "But
there's someplace else I need to be."

He didn't take kindly to being dismissed. "Big talk for a
skinny bitch who doesn't know any better than to be out
this time of night by herself."

He'd only glanced briefly over his shoulder toward the
new voice, probably immediately dismissing it as a threat
to his spontaneous plan because it belonged to a woman.
His second mistake of the night.

He blinked when Louisa easily slipped her hand from
his hold. When he realized she was getting away, Mr.
Manners grunted and pushed into her space, even more
aggressive and smelling of expensive booze and previous
bad decisions.

She took a step away from him and he followed, his
hand snapping up to clamp around her arm and digging into
skin through her coat. Amused laughter rippled from the
alley and Louisa dismissed any thought that the woman
would come to her rescue; not that she needed it.

She whipped her knee up, sharp and hard, to smash into
the man's balls. She didn't look at him as he dropped
heavily to the sidewalk, mewling in pain. "Fucking bitch!"

"A bit of a one-note, isn't he?" The woman stepped out
of the alley, the yellow streetlight finding unfamiliar,

silver-tipped blue hair. But her face, all sharp lines and obsidian skin, was one Louisa knew very well. "It's bitch this and bitch that," she said. "He could at least throw in a cunt or slag once in a while. Broaden his misogynistic vocabulary."

The sight of Damali pulled a quiet sigh from Louisa. Damn, she was breathtaking! This was the woman she'd had dreams of on and off for years, a dangerous and thrilling influence she'd compared all other lovers to. She looked dressed for a productive night in a sleek weatherproof jumpsuit and thick-soled boots that were silent against the pavement. The gloves she wore didn't look thick enough for the weather. Still, Louisa's mouth dried just from the sight of her.

"People don't say 'slag' in this country," Louisa said for want of anything pertinent to add. Her brain was still settling around the fact that Damali was in New York and not on some sun-splashed European terrace with a dildo strapped to her hips and hot intention in her eyes. Like the last time they had been this close.

Damali shrugged. "No loss there." She gathered the straps of a cloth backpack and pulled them over her shoulder. "You ready?"

"For what?"

"There's a diner you'd like that's not too far from here." She jerked her head toward the next street.

"Sure. I'm game." Louisa walked past a groaning Mr. Manners and fell in step with the woman who'd once been both her dream and her nightmare.

At the all-night diner, Louisa ordered hot chocolate with a shot of espresso. It felt like she was putting Damali in her mouth. That outer edge of sweet that masked the adrenaline pumping infusion that this woman had always brought to her life.

"What are you doing in New York?"

She didn't address the fact that the last time they had seen each other was in Barcelona, a lazy weekend fuck that had turned into a week running wild through the city and nearly getting thrown in jail. Good times. She should have been nervous that Damali had known exactly where in the city she was. Damali was a paid killer who very much loved her job. But Louisa knew there were worse things to be afraid of.

"I'm doing some work here in the city for a few days," Damali said with a shrug. "Nothing big."

"Nothing big" for her could mean just about anything. From collecting a package to taking out an entire street full of armed men. Damali took everything as the same. No job or situation, no matter the size, stressed her out. Maybe it was the reason Louisa was half in love with her, and had been since they met on a Spanish summer vacation almost fifteen years before, two teenage girls on neighboring luxury properties with not enough legal entertainment to occupy their felonious little minds.

"Sounds like fun of the usual kind," Louisa said. Her chocolate was hot, almost too hot. She held it between her hands to keep the cold at bay.

"It *will* be fun," Damali said. "Want to help?" She held the question in her mouth like a challenge.

Louisa's eyebrow rose. She could never back away from a challenge. "Sure. What do you want me to do?"

"Just be yourself."

"What? Bored?"

Damali grinned, baring her sharp canines. "Are you bored right now?"

"Yeah, actually." That was a lie. Her heartbeat was racing under her couture dress. Life in New York could get stagnant at times, except when she livened it up with a bit of high-end burglary with some old friends good enough to never get caught. Otherwise, she was a bored semi-socialite. One with enough money to do the coveted celebrity-filled parties and charity events. Right now, though, she wasn't bored. But it was too late to take it back. Damali was grinning like a mad thing and reaching across the table to pull Louisa to her feet.

"Come on then," she said. "Let's find something to make that sweet little pulse of yours race."

Louisa knew she was going to regret her false confession of boredom, but the part of her that didn't give a damn about rules or a little spilled blood grinned right back. "Let's go."

They ended up in NoHo. Staring down at the loft of one of the celebrities Damali had a crush on. Some B-list hipster queer who recently landed himself a boy toy nearly half his age. Louisa loved reading about him in the paper. It made her feel a connection with Damali who occasionally sent emails from halfway around the world with tidbits about her crush's life in New York. Damali may or may not have been stalking him.

She was the one who'd sent Louisa the email about the new multimillion dollar loft he'd bought with his new boyfriend. They squatted on the roof of a nearby building, binoculars trained on the loft and the men inside. The boy toy was smoking in the window, pretty and willowy with his Diana Ross hair blowing in the cold breeze. The one Damali was obsessed with lay on the couch reading a thick collection of papers, maybe a script.

"What are we doing here?"

"Curing your boredom." Damali teased her with another teeth-baring grin. "Isn't that what you said, kitten? That you were bored."

She didn't wait for Louisa to answer, just grabbed her hand and yanked her to her feet. "Come relieve your ennui with me." They scrambled back down the side of the building and crossed the near silent street to stare up at the six story lofted apartment. Damali shot a grappling hook up at the building and yanked the rope until it properly anchored on the edge of the empty roof. "Come." She turned her back. "Climb on."

Louisa didn't give herself the chance to say no. But wasn't this how she ended up outside a New York nightclub being amateur-assaulted by an idiot who didn't know better than to molest strange women? She latched herself to Damali who pressed a button on the gun-like barrel of the grappling hook. The hook whirred to life, lifting them slowly toward the roof. The cold air bit into Louisa's exposed cheeks as they rose. She kept her eyes wide open, her arms wrapped tightly around Damali's waist. Even through all the layers, she felt the heat of her body. The woman was a damn furnace. Every time Louisa was with her, she knew she would get burned.

The furnished rooftop was like most Louisa had visited before, decked out with elegant waterproof patio furniture in shades of white and brown, potted trees, and a pair of red-stained wine glasses left out on a low table. She still felt out of place.

"Maybe I should have dressed more appropriately for this."

"I don't know about that." Damali looked her up and down with familiar heat. "I think you look more than fine." She stepped close to Louisa with her smile on full blast. "Were you hurt? Did you survive the ride in one piece?" Again, she didn't wait for answers, just skimmed her hands down Louisa's neck, over her coat to grope her ass and legs, a pat-down that was more of a filthy subway feel-up. "Hm. You feel just fine to me."

"Somehow, I don't think you're qualified to determine that."

Damali shrugged. "I'm wounded you don't trust me."

Trust had never been something between them. After all, wasn't Damali the one who'd abandoned Louisa in the bathroom of a girl's boarding school after convincing her to sneak in so they could have a three way with a millionaire's virgin daughter? Never mind that it had been one of the most exhilarating experiences of Louisa's life. To this day, her family never let her forget it. The shame for Louisa was in getting caught. She never made that mistake again.

"Come on," she said to Damali. "Let's get whatever you came here for."

The boys were on the top floor of the six-story building. Relaxing in front of the fire and enjoying a night in from the cold. Damali strode across the roof, hips rocking underneath a tight black jumpsuit more suited to a ski lodge than a night of breaking and entering. Louisa followed in her stilettos and party dress feeling severely over-dressed.

They dropped down onto the fire escape, Louisa following Damali's lead as she slid open a window and climbed into the loft that was decorated in layer upon layer of white. The sound of the television murmured from down the hall while music piped in from another room.

"Do humans even live here?" Louisa whispered as she crept across the hardwood floors on her tip toes, trying not to make noise in her spiked heels. "Who decorates in all white? It's like a Clorox commercial."

Damali brushed a gloved hand over a white leather chair. "Hmm. It's just begging for a little splash of red." Her teeth bared in a terrifying smile.

No. She wouldn't. Would she?

Louisa glanced down the hall to where the movie star was draped on the couch being boring on a Saturday night, but Damali led her in another direction, away from the boys. Never one to shy away from a little B & E, Louisa absolutely drew the line at murder. Maybe. Sometimes she wasn't sure where her morality lay. Her feelings weren't exactly *feelings,* but she knew who she cared about, like naïve but fun Reyna and her new conventional life, and she would kill for them without hesitation.

"What would you do…" Damali quietly asked in her most bored and uninterested voice. "…if I killed them both right now?"

The boys were talking now, something about a party where one of them had run into a former co-star. Despite her apparent indifference, Louisa could tell Damali was excited to be near her crush. She thought he was gorgeous and fuckable, despite her abhorrence of even the suggestion of sex with men. She'd never hurt him.

"Is that even a real question?" Louisa shook her head and walked away, continuing in the direction they'd been heading. Seconds later, Damali came up behind her, quiet in her boots and passed Louisa after squeezing her butt cheek in a tight grip. It hurt. But the pain sent a jolt straight between Louisa's legs.

She shook it off and followed.

They slipped into a guest room on quiet feet. In the smaller of the two bedrooms, Damali traced her gloved fingers around a faint outline of a door, a little pressure and it slid open as quietly as a sigh.

Louisa stared at it in amazement, wondering if the celebrity couple knew about it. Damali disappeared through the door and yanked her in behind her. A huff of surprise escaped Louisa's parted lips just as the door shut at her back.

They stepped into darkness. Then a wide circle of light from a flashlight in Damali's hand illuminated the unexpected room. They were in a small closet, probably the dimensions of some poor soul's studio apartment not very far from where they stood. The walls were bare, the floor naked hardwood.

Damali, apparently the hidden-door whisperer, immediately found a narrow square outlined in the floor. It clicked open and up under the pressure of her hands. She gestured for Louisa to go down first. Louisa didn't hesitate.

She braced her hands on the sides of the small opening and climbed down when her feet found the rungs of a ladder. Damali followed her into a small room identical to the one they'd just left, immediately going for the door her flashlight revealed. She put some kind of device, black and the size of a matchbox, against the door and listened for a moment, then gestured for Louisa the same time the door opened and sprung out.

Louisa went, and stumbled outside the door then it whispered closed behind her. She turned to ask Damali "what next?" But she was alone. The wall was smooth as if there was no door at all.

What the fuck?

But she knew better than to say it out loud even when a thick male voice echoed her confusion.

"What the fuck?" A slender man in all black stared at her. His eyes widened just as he reached for the gun in his waistband. Louisa stumbled back into the wall, hissed as her ankle turned painfully in the high heels.

145

"Hey..." She tried for a smile as two men barreled past the man toward her, guns drawn. Her stomach clenched in panic and she mentally cursed the Australian woman to hell and back. The two men, six-footers with impressively intimidating snarls, grabbed her arms and shook her between them.

"Who are you and what the fuck are you doing here?" It was the thin man who spoke.

"I just stumbled down here from the fire escape." She raised her hands. "This is just some sort of huge mistake."

"A mistake my ass."

More like *my* ass, Louisa thought with a rising panic that almost felt like excitement, breath deepening, her nipples tightening under her coat. Would this be a repeat of the French boarding school incident, every burglar for herself?

Hands dug into her arms through the coat. But the coat didn't last long. The men dragged it off her and tossed it aside, yanked off her scarf, plucked the pins from her hair and felt her up through the dress. Not as nice as what Damali had done nearly half an hour before. She hoped they wouldn't follow up the grope with a more thorough search involving their dicks. Her spine yanked straight at the thought.

"I was on the fire escape smoking. I thought I was climbing back into my friend's place." Unlikely but better than the truth.

"What the fuck do you take us for? Idiots?"

"Not at all. Just sensible men who don't want to do anything rash," she said.

They snorted like twin bulls and dragged her through the loft—not decorated in all white, thank God—to the main room where she was roughly presented to a monster of a man reclining on a sofa. He was big, broad, and pasty, propped up on dark leather cushions, watching something on TV. Apparently it was the night to be up and watching television. Didn't people in New York have more exciting lives than this?

"This is who was making all that noise, boss."

Even the damn bodyguards had bodyguards. The ones who'd dragged her through the loft stepped back a few feet to do their best impression of wallpaper. The thin man was the one to present her in front of the boss.

He slapped her hard with a bony hand, pushing her to her knees. Despite her determination to stay cool, her heart began to drum fiercely in her chest. This had the potential to not end well. For her.

The boss looked her up and down, from her loosened hair to the dress that had seemed fine before she left the house but now felt a little risqué for thug interrogation. She wanted to yank the thing up to her neck and reach somewhere back in time for a nun's habit. His eyes on her made her skin crawl. He shifted his feet in front of him on the couch but did not get up.

"Why are you here?"

"I told you, I—" The slap to the face knocked her sideways. Luckily her new friends were there to catch her. The taste of blood exploded in her mouth.

"I won't ask you nice again."

Well, my sometimes fuck buddy tossed me down here to entertain you while she does something I'm not exactly sure what.

That didn't sound like something she could say to avoid another punch so she kept the comment behind her teeth. Louisa spat the blood on the bare hardwood. Just in time to catch a punch in the face. Pain and a gasping breath jerked out of her.

Fuck...

Not a damn loose tooth? She poked her tongue against her front teeth, then quietly sighed in relief. Okay. False alarm. But it wouldn't hurt to make an appointment with her dentist on Monday morn—

A switchblade snicked open near her ear, cutting off her thought. "I think we're treating her too nice, boss."

Louisa flinched from where she thought the blade was. She hated knives. And she didn't like the sound of "too nice."

"Fuck!"

This time, she couldn't keep quiet when another punch slammed into her stomach. She was almost thankful the giants were there to hold her up, otherwise she would've collapsed on her rubbery legs. It was the little things.

"Now is that any way to treat a lady?"

Louisa had never been so glad to hear Damali's voice in her life. The Australian didn't give them a chance to respond. The men at Louisa's sides jerked like a puppet master yanked their strings. Their heads flung back and they dropped on the floor, each with two shots, one to the head and another to the heart. Louisa noticed all this while her own heart raced. A flash appeared in her peripheral vision and then the slender man was dead, red splashing out of him, the stink of his voiding bowels filling the room. Another flash and the man on the sofa slumped sideways. Four dead men in less than ten seconds.

Shock dropped Louisa on her ass. Sprawled out in front of her, her legs were too weak to do more than tremble. Her stilettos sounded like they were tap-dancing across the hardwood floor. "Shit!"

She was frightened out of her damn mind, on the verge of pissing herself, which was not something she preferred to do. Outside the bathroom, and the occasional well-prepared bedroom, the smell of urine was not something she wanted to experience.

Louisa wasn't thinking, she was only feeling panic and anger at having to visit the dentist when she wasn't even due for another checkup for four months. That was the only reason she flew across the room and slapped Damali across the face. Hard. She raised her hand again to come back for more, but Damali caught her wrist in a bruising grip.

"That first one was free," she said. "The next one is going to cost you."

Growling, Louisa clenched her fist, getting ready to make it count. But Damali smiled, blinding and white as if she didn't just threaten her.

"Breathe, baby. It's all right. You were great." She turned the imprisonment of Louisa's wrist into a caress, dragging her fingers down the delicate bones of her hand, her shoulder, the bloodied black silk of the dress. By the time those fingers slid down Louisa's side, trailing over the swell of her breast, a different emotion entirely was making her shiver.

Not this. Not now.

But it *was* right now. Her mouth was desert dry with one look from Damali.

"Were you scared, baby?" Her voice scraped over Louisa's raw nerves, making her instantly and achingly wet.

What the fuck was this woman doing to her? She may or may not have asked herself that question the same moment Damali dropped to her knees. "You were so good for me," she said, pressing her face into Louisa's lap and inhaling deeply. "So good."

She dragged up Louisa's skirt and Louisa let her, frozen to the spot while Damali yanked up her skirt the rest of the way and slid her fingers past the edge of her panties.

"You dirty, dirty thing."

There was nothing Louisa could do to hide what she was feeling. The sound of Damali's fingers inside her was a loud squelch, liquid. Not just moisture but soaking wet enough for her to shove her whole hand up Louisa's pussy with no prep. Well, maybe not that wet, but close enough.

"You know I love this." Damali hummed. "I love that you're game for anything." Her fingers shoved deeper in Louisa's pussy and Louisa shivered where she stood, widening her legs, letting Damali do what she wanted. "I could fuck you here in the middle of all these dead cunts and you'd love it, wouldn't you?"

No.

She meant to say no, but it came out as a gasp as Damali finally touched her clit, stroked it with her thumb while her eyes held Louisa captive. This wasn't the role Louisa played, ever.

With women, she was always in control. And with men too. They kneeled before her and sucked her off until she told them to stop. She rode them and got off before they could even think of coming. She was the one who wielded the strap-on and fucked them until they screamed for her to never stop or to stop or just screamed her name.

But she couldn't do anything while Damali fucked her. She could only watch her brown eyes, implacable and undeniable, the way she licked her lips in satisfaction, moving her fingers in Louisa's pussy at her own leisure. Damali may have been on her knees but she was the one with all the power. Louisa's eyes fluttered shut.

"No. Keep your eyes open. I want you to see this. I want you to know who's fucking you." But even though Louisa opened her eyes and kept them open, Damali pulled her fingers from her pussy and licked them, sliding the two obscenely into her mouth and licking the glistening wetness from them.

Louisa's knees trembled. She wanted to just fall to the ground and let it be over, just open her mouth and beg Damali to fuck her, because that was where she always ended up with this woman. Begging and on her back. Always begging, always wanting.

Damali rose to her feet, graceful in her black clothes. Louisa kept her eyes on her. It was easier than looking at the dead men around her, their blood splashing the walls and the furniture, the smell of death that she'd always suspected but had never known.

"Bend over the chair. I want to see your pussy." Damali was breathless. She hurriedly unzipped her one piece suit but left it on, the zipper parting down the middle to show off another layer beneath it, a practical concern for the cold. She shoved her hands in her panties and roughly fingered herself. "I *said*—," when Louisa took too long. "—bend over the chair."

There were three chairs in the room, but Louisa knew she meant the one where the man had been sitting before. Now he was lying sideways in it, his eyes staring out at nothing. Louisa shouldn't have been so eager, but *God*, she was. She fell onto her belly across the back of the leather couch, her dress dragged up her thighs and over her ass. The leather was cold on her stomach.

"Fuck, you're so damn nice." Damali's mouth latched onto her pussy and began to eat her with a savagery that pulled whimpers of pleasure from Louisa's throat.

It was a mouth she knew, a rhythm she loved. She'd almost forgotten. *Fuck!* Her eyes squeezed tight and her mouth opened wide and she screamed loud enough to wake the dead men around them as Damali lashed her clit, rammed her tongue deep into her. Then it was two fingers inside, slamming into her and Damali's mouth sucking on her clit.

Louisa was a whore for it. She loved it. She wanted it. She yanked down the top of her dress and shoved back, wriggled until the leather was pressed into her breasts and the ravenous motions of Damali's mouth and fingers pushed her back and forth on the leather, rubbing her nipples to hard points, bringing even more heat to her pussy.

She came screaming.

Panting, she turned around on weakened legs to see Damali still working herself through the parted zipper of her fancy onesie. Her pupils were blown wide with arousal. She jerked her hand, a rough thrust of her fingers. Damali's eyes flashed with impatience. She'd always been a hard come, eager to fuck in new and dangerous places but inevitably needing more than a few minutes to reach her climax, even with her own fingers. She yanked her hand from her pussy.

"Make me come," Damali demanded, her mouth wet with Louisa's juices. "You know how I like it."

Louisa stepped close, hands ready to tug the one piece suit down to get better access, but Damali shook her head, her blue and silver hair flying over her shoulders. "Just like this."

A challenge. Okay.

Louisa shoved Damali back into the wall. Damali fucked her lovers the way she wanted to be fucked, rough and thorough. They didn't have time for the second one, but Louisa would definitely make time for the first. She squeezed Damali's breasts through the layers of cloth, searching for the hard nipple.

"Just fuck me already!"

Louisa jammed her hand into the crotch of the suit, found her pussy hairs soaked, her hole slick and tempting. She pinched her clit and Damali cried out.

"Harder."

Then she shoved her fingers, wet from her own juices, into Louisa's mouth and Louisa gasped around them, quickly got with the program and sucked at the salty taste and the faint hint of steel. She shoved a hand up Damali's shirt to get at her breasts, squeezed a nipple while her other hand pinched and pulled at her fat clit.

The angle was hard and any moment now her wrist was going to start hurting. But for now it was damn near magic with Damali's impatient fingers sliding over her tongue and the gasping groan she let go as Louisa dragged her closer to orgasm. But even this wasn't enough. She needed something else. She needed…

Louisa growled and dropped to her knees, grabbed the knife that had been nudging her foot while they fucked. She grinned with wild satisfaction at Damali's gasp of surprise when she cut open the pants, ripped the panties, got it wide enough for her to get her hand at the better angle. And *God* that was the best decision she'd ever made. She clicked the knife shut and shoved it into the top of her dress with one hand while the other fucked Damali.

She stood up, pressed Damali's face away, pushing her cheek into the wall, covering her face with her fingers spread wide. Damali hated to be kissed when they were fucking. And Louisa was more than happy to give her what she wanted, as long as she kept coming back for more, even if it was every two years or so. She licked her neck, sucked the skin over her strumming pulse.

Damali wasn't much of a talker when she was getting hers during sex. But her body spoke for her, the quivering of breath in her throat, the hard clench of her jaw, the way her hips fucked up into Louisa's fingers.

Damali shuddered hard against the wall, and Louisa could feel from the tremor in her thighs, that she was hovering right there, ready to come. But then she felt the intensity recede. A good tongue would make Louisa come faster than anything. But this was Damali, she always needed something a little extra.

It was desperation that made her grab the knife out of her cleavage. She rubbed her thumb over Damali's clit, then slid the rounded knife handle into her pussy.

"What are you...? Fuck..." Damali's voice trailed off on an open-mouthed sob. She blinked frantically at the ceiling, swallowing loudly.

155

Louisa worked the knife like her favorite tiny dildo, dipping its curved handle in and searching up for her gush spot. Damali's fists thumped into the wall and her thighs opened wider, trembling in the ragged remnants of her suit. Her dripping pussy swallowed the bone handle of the knife, squeezing and releasing around it.

"Fucking...Christ!" Damali's entire body vibrated. A wild breath shot from her throat then she was jerking as if caught in an electrical current. "Shit..." Her blue-tipped silver hair was stuck to the sweat on her face, strands caught in her mouth and blowing out with each breath.

Louisa licked her neck and slowly withdrew the knife. "Good?"

"Fuck." Damali grabbed her and kissed her roughly, sucking her tongue, biting her lips. "You're bloody amazing."

"So I've been told." She tucked the knife back in her cleavage. Definitely keeping it as a souvenir.

Damali pulled back to look into her face. "Oh yeah. I bet you have plenty of people panting after that pretty pussy of yours."

"Enough to keep things interesting."

"Yeah. I bet." Damali licked her lips like she was savoring the taste of what they'd done. "We need to get out of here before their backup gets here." She looked down at her ripped pants and cursed.

Louisa smirked and tugged down her dress, already looking around for her coat and everything else she came with. "What about the cops?"

"That's the least of our worries." Damali arranged the crotch of her pants the best way she could, grabbed her guns and the backpack that was swollen with something that hadn't been in it before. "Let's go."

Louisa tried her best not to look at any of the men they passed, or more precisely, their bodies, as she and Damali made their way back to the hidden door. Damali quickly got it open, hustled them into the studio-closet then, after listening to make sure her favorite boy was nowhere near their exit, pushed open the last door into the all-white apartment.

The boys were together on the couch now, the actor still reading his script but his boy toy—maybe his love for life?—had his head in his lap. Tender fingers combed through the thick wavy hair. From what Louisa could see as she passed, they looked content. Maybe the naysayers and haters were wrong. Maybe he *had* found a lasting love with his twink. Love didn't always look like high school sweethearts exchanging promise rings.

Their life together was seductive with its normalcy. But as good as it looked, and she could admit she found it appealing, something like that wasn't for her. She turned her back on the boys to follow Damali back uptown and to her hotel to change clothes, fuck in a proper bed, then say goodbye until the next time they met.

Later, when Damali had her tied up and with the handle of a wooden hairbrush sticking out of her ass, her butt cheeks stinging from slaps, Louisa thought about her friend away on her honeymoon, she thought about the celebrities in their loft, and about how far she was from that kind of domestic contentment. Maybe all she deserved was this. The sex and the danger and the blood. Everything else was too sweet for someone like her. Too far out of reach. So she closed her eyes and sank into the sharp pleasure Damali gave and felt it as deeply as she could. Until the next time.

"Vicissitudes"

The morning after Rowan proposed to Alma, he woke up transformed, his body turned into a woman's. Change must have stolen over him during the night, softening masculine flesh, smoothing away the rough bass of his voice. Something made Rowan keep still after the initial shift against the sheets, sheets that clung to limbs that felt lighter, to hips that curved and made her want to curl her body inward and continue with sleep. But wetness woke her up. Blood.

Ro, a different version of Rowan, felt it sticky and cooling between her thighs and under her hips in the bed. It'd been so long since she felt it but this was unmistakably her period. *Her* period. She wanted to jump up in the bed, shock at her sudden femaleness making it nearly impossible to stay still. But she wasn't alone.

Alma.

The night before, it had rained. A light spring shower to wash the island clean. Rowan had left the window open and turned off the air conditioning. Now, the smell of rain-battered flowers and wet earth eased into the room. Outside, Ro imagined the red hibiscus flowers bowed shut, only their long pistils with the dusting of pollen poking beyond the fire red petals. In the bed, she slowly turned.

The first thing Ro saw was Alma's cheek, the soft brown skin wrinkled from the sheets. The thick wing of an eyebrow. Her mouth hidden by the pillow. Rowan's

fiancée—was she anything else since Rowan was now
gone?—sighed into her pillow and moved closer.
Please. Please, don't wake up.

Even as she pleaded silently for Alma to stay sheltered
in sleep, Ro welcomed her intrusion into her personal
space. She didn't move closer although part of her wanted
to bury herself in the soft comfort of Alma and her delicate
woman's body. But that wasn't a choice she had. Ro
smelled something else. She smelled herself. The blood, the
womaness, thick like a truth she couldn't deny.

But why? Why did the change come now?

She knew the answer. Last night's happiness had
flashed through her, a fireburst, too intense to be safe. A
gendermorph's physical changes, her mother always
warned her, were triggered by extreme emotions, or acute
physical changes. Ro had known better than to try for
happiness, but she dared anyway.

She crawled out of the bed, careful not to wake Alma.
For once, glad Rowan's fiancée was a heavy sleeper.
Keeping her thighs pressed together, Ro rushed to the
bathroom, turned the shower on "hot," and jumped in
without giving the water a chance to heat up. She made
quick work of it, washing down her entire body, thoroughly
cleaning the crevices, the curves, deliberately not lingering
to explore the familiar yet foreign body with its unrelenting
crimson drops. Alma was waiting. Alma would wonder.

Ro finished in the shower and pulled on a robe—unable
to face the glimpses of her naked self, even in the misted
mirror—then rummaged through Alma's drawer until she

found a tampon and, after several painful attempts, fully inserted it. Her womb throbbed with faint pain. Ro closed the toilet, sat down on the lid, trembling in the thin cotton robe.

She wanted to break things. In the mirror, her reflection moved. Still, Ro avoided looking directly at it. She wasn't ready. Instead, she stared down at her fingers, slim and fragile looking. They quivered against her thighs.

Last night had been the night Rowan was finally able to let go of his fears and face the happiness that could be his with Alma, the only woman who'd ever mattered. And now any chance of that happiness was gone. Escaped like the blood staining the bed sheets in the next room.

Alma.

"Alma."

Ro flinched, surprised at her soft woman's voice. The last time she'd heard it, she was thirteen years old and the change only lasted three weeks. Long enough for Rowan to miss a noticeable amount of school and for their mother to explain essential female things to Ro. Essential things for her to know when or *if* her female self came back for good.

Ro squirmed from her seat on top of the toilet. She couldn't keep herself cooped up in the bathroom like a prisoner. Well, she could, but it would be weird. She swallowed. Then, after quickly hanging the robe on the back of the bathroom door, crept into the quiet bedroom.

Alma still slept. Curled like a snail toward Rowan's place in the bed, one elbow tucked into her stomach, cheek resting in her open palm on the pillow. Near her legs, the blood stain sat like an accusation.

Ro stared at the woman she loved, and something inside her turned, something sharp and painful, a tightening screw. It was the awareness that Rowan might not ever touch her again, that he would miss out on the chance to breathe next to her, to make love with her again. Tears started, and she couldn't stop them. On the bed, Alma twitched and made a soft noise. Ro quickly wiped her face.

This was the last change.

It felt final. Alma lost to her forever while she stood firmly in the curves, in the awareness, she would have until the day she died.

Cowardice and fear made her grab Rowan's discarded jeans and T-shirt from the floor and slip from the room. Once out of the bedroom, she could actually think again, her mind clear of the scent of Alma or her own blood. She remembered now the soreness Rowan had felt in his chest and hips over the past few weeks, a dull ache that he thought had been from him simply working out too hard, running too much, lifting too many weights. Now, breathing in her female body, Ro realized it had been the transformation all along, slyly preparing Rowan for Ro. She yanked on the clothes.

At the kitchen sink, she splashed cold water on her face, getting ready to walk out and walk off the panic. But—

"Rowan?"

Ro stiffened at the sound of Alma's voice, close. She twisted the spigot shut and quick-walked toward the back door but only made it as far as the stove when Alma walked in, gorgeously naked, hair like a dandelion cloud around her face but smashed down on one side, the most beautiful woman in Jamaica. She blinked when she saw Ro.

She stopped short, blushing, started backing out of the kitchen and covering her nakedness with her hands at the same time.

"Oh, I'm sorry! I didn't know anyone else was here." But in the same amount of time it took her to say those words, her eyes narrowed with suspicion, her nudity forgotten in the face of Ro's unfamiliar presence. "Can I help you?" Her voice was sharp. "Does Rowan know you're here?"

Ro turned to face her, a clenched fist on the edge of the cold stove. She cleared her throat. "Yes, he does."

Again, she was surprised at the sound of her own voice, husky and low, but undoubtedly feminine. She cleared her throat again as Alma grabbed a dish towel, using its flimsy protection to half-cover her body. Rowan's fiancée walked deeper into the kitchen, eyes still narrowed with suspicion. She and Rowan had talked before about people who sometimes roamed up and down their lane, crazy people who could break into your house if you were careless enough to leave the door open for even a moment. Lunatics who would kill easily, their consciences smothered in madness.

Ro pressed back against the stove as Alma came closer with her big eyes and the diamond engagement ring on her finger. The ring made Ro ache even more for everything she'd lost during the night.

Alma's eyes widened after a moment. "You...are you—?" Her question tumbled away into uncertainty. "You look so much like Rowan," Alma said, her voice suddenly trembling, her fierceness falling away like paper armor.

"He's my brother," Ro said, forcing the lie past her teeth. Rowan and Alma never lied to each other. Never.

But this lie made sense. There was nothing else for her to say. Why else was she in Rowan's house in the early morning?

Alma hovered in the doorway, her small dishtowel drifting between her breasts and the furred triangle at the tops of her thighs, hiding very little. "I didn't know he had a sister, or any siblings."

"Just me," Ro said, getting distracted by what was above and below the kitchen towel despite the other things on her mind. "I'm sorry to intrude on your morning." Her eyes dropped low, lingering on any bit of soft skin, every curve that caught and held the glow of early morning sunlight.

"I..." Alma yanked the flimsy kitchen towel back up to her chest. "Excuse me!" She backed out of the kitchen.

Ro breathed a relieved breath and pushed out of the kitchen door to make her escape. Every second spent in Alma's presence felt like a test. One she was failing. She had to leave, but where could she go?

It was a Saturday. A rest day.

The only person she could think to turn to was Nelson. Crass but kind, he was the closest thing Rowan had to a best friend. He lived just a short walk away. The two had known each other since their freshman year at the University of the West Indies in Kingston.

Barefoot, Ro made her way to his house, mud grabbing at the bottoms of her jeans, squishing up between her toes.

At Nelson's house, she knocked on the door and stepped back.

"Hold on, hold on!" A voice came from just behind the door, then the rattling release of the key on the other side.

"What the fuck are you doing here? Shouldn't you be having newly engaged sex all over that big bed you—". The door had steadily opened during Nelson's half-muttered greeting. In the doorway, he scrubbed his eyes with the heel of one hand and scratched his balls through loose pajama pants.

But when he really focused on Ro, his monologue stopped.

"Fuck me! I thought you were somebody else." Then he shook his head. "Shit, you look so much like... anyway." He straightened and attempted a welcoming smile. "Good morning, miss. How can I help you?"

Ro almost laughed. She could count on one hand the times she'd heard Nelson referred to a woman as "miss."

"Just let me in," Ro said. She'd considered and quickly discarded the idea of lying to him, feeding him the bullshit story about a visiting sister, but it felt like too much. She pushed into the front room and found her way to his

165

kitchen and the fancy coffee maker he was unnaturally attached to. "I need booze," Ro said. "But coffee will have to do."

"Hey!" Nelson barreled in after her. "It's not that I don't appreciate such a lovely—" Despite the situation, Ro choked on a laugh. "—woman so early in the morning barging into my home to make me coffee, but who the fuck are you?"

Ro started the coffee machine, grabbed her favorite cup from the dish rack where Rowan put it last time he was there.

"First off, I'm making *myself* coffee. You can have some if you want." She braced her hands on either side of the coffee maker, watching the dark liquid drip, her personal Zen waterfall. Then she turned, and caught Nelson looking at her ass. She shook her head. "Second, I'm Rowan's other half."

Nelson stood in the doorway of his small kitchen, arms crossed over his bare chest. "I'm damn sure I know who Rowan's girlfriend is, and it's not you."

His gaze dipped low on Ro's body and she let him. "As delusions go, you can do better. At least imagine a single guy as your boyfriend, like me." He rubbed his chest with a slow smile.

"If this is how you try to get women, no wonder you hardly get any ass," Ro muttered. "Do you want some of this coffee?"

Nelson nodded, probably by reflex, then he was staring at her with his fish-out-of-water look, mouth gaping, eyes big. Ro grabbed his cup too and plunked it on the counter beside her own. The coffee dripped into the silence.

"I'm Rowan," she said. "At least I was."

Nelson shut his mouth and looked intrigued. It was one of the things Rowan had liked immediately about him when they met. Despite his perpetually filthy mouth and love of American gangster movies, Nelson was open-minded, not the typical macho Jamaican man.

Given his degree in biotechnology, he was a good observer, took in a situation before making judgments, and never let anyone else or even previously understood truths get in the way of him finding his way to a new one.

Ro could practically *feel* him analyzing what was in front of him: Ro coming into his house and knowing precisely where everything was, knowing how to work the machine that was as unnecessarily complicated as it was magical. And then there was her face.

"This is awkward," Nelson said finally. "I never thought I'd get a boner for the female version of you." He adjusted himself in his pants.

Ro made a sound of annoyance. "Get yourself under control."

The coffee finished brewing and she made them each a cup, with a splash of hazelnut flavor the way Nelson liked. Her own coffee, cream and no sugar, soothed something of her unease, but it was only a surface solution.

Her skin still felt tight around her bones, too delicate and unfamiliar after all these years of being Rowan. It was no wonder Nelson couldn't stop looking at her.

167

Although Ro had come first, then slipped away three weeks after being born, Rowan had never made peace with her. He'd fought fiercely for his survival, for his maleness, taking the most masculine job (engineer at a top biotech firm), finding the most macho friends, staying in Jamaica although it would have become trouble if—*when*—he became female again and continued dating women.

But ironically as he'd grown older and memories of being Ro faded away to nearly nothing, he tempered his hyper-masculinity. Stopped trying to fuck anything with a pussy, admitted that he didn't give a shit about football, allowed himself pleasure in small things – rainy nights, a face next to his on the pillow, cooking for the woman he loved. And of all the brutes he'd befriended, only Nelson remained.

"This is weird as fuck," Nelson said. He looked at Ro over the edge of his coffee mug.

"Imagine how I feel."

"I'd rather not, thanks." Nelson slurped his coffee, pronounced it perfect, then gestured for Ro to follow him up to the rooftop terrace. "How are you going to tell Alma?"

Because, of course, it never occurred to him that Ro wouldn't tell Alma about this very important development. He knew how much Rowan loved Alma. Hurting her with an unexplained disappearance, especially after their recent engagement, wasn't something Rowan would ever do.

"I told her I'm Rowan's sister."

Nelson gave her his "you idiot" look.

On the terrace that was still wet from last night's rain, Ro wiped water off the iron bench before she sat down. "I should just leave. Tell her Rowan died or something…" Dampness seeped into her jeans and the back of her T-shirt.

"That's the stupidest idea you've ever had," Nelson said. "And believe me, you've had a few."

"Rowan probably won't come back. What else am I supposed to do?"

Ro was a mess of hormones and hesitations, sadness and shock. Every decision felt like too much, while at the same time, not enough. Every escape seemed like another prison. She gulped the hot coffee.

"Maybe you're right." Nelson splashed bare feet through the standing water, peered over the edge of the terrace to the bright garden and green hills below. "You should leave. I'll take care of Alma's needs and comforts until you get back."

He leaned back against the balcony with one hand braced on the metal railing, the other raising the coffee cup to his smirking mouth.

The anger shot through Ro hot and fast, a relief after all the uncertainty. "If you touch her you'll never use your dick again, not even to piss." She growled, low and savage.

But Nelson only laughed at her. "And what are you going to do about it once you make like Houdini out of her life? You may be a chick now, but you better man up and tell her what happened. Give *her* the chance to tell you to fuck off."

"I don't think—"

169

A sound behind Nelson had him turning around to look over his shoulder. "Looks like you'll get your chance sooner than you think." He looked at Ro, an eyebrow raised. "Or at least sooner than you would like."

Then Ro heard it too, footsteps up the gravel walk. Then Alma's voice called out.

"Hey, Nelson!"

He turned to wave his mug at Alma, smiling wide. "Morning!"

"Have you seen Rowan?" she asked.

"Not this morning, but his sister is right here. Come on up!"

"You motherfucker…"

"That's not very lady-like." Nelson snorted in his coffee. "I'm going to put on some clothes and head out after I let her in." He turned to make sure Alma was coming up, then headed toward the stairs. "Good luck," he threw over his shoulder almost as an afterthought.

When he left, Ro sat, frozen. She turned the warm coffee mug around and around in her hands. The slender fingers resting against the burgundy ceramic of the cup were so alien, the narrow wrists, the delicate bones just beneath the skin. But the thin scar—from a straight razor shaving experiment gone wrong—still sliced across the back of her hand. It was as familiar as her left handed grip, and the crooked middle finger that had never healed properly from its break nearly five years before.

She tensed at the sound of Alma's footsteps coming up the stairs, but she stayed where she was, waiting. Ro thought she was ready, but Alma's appearance felt like a punch to the throat. It left her gasping quietly, trying to catch her breath. She put the coffee cup at her feet, unable to hold it in her trembling hands.

Alma wore one of her simple dresses, one that Rowan always teased her was as easy to pull off as it was to put on. Yellow. Old fashioned. Narrow at the waist and with a single zipper down the back. She looked like sunlight.

"Hello again." Alma hovered at the entrance to the terrace, one foot on the last stair, her hands braced on the walls on either side of her. "Nelson said you had something to tell me." Her voice was soft, hesitant.

"No, it's—"

"If you're getting ready to tell me a lie," Alma cut her off. "I don't want to hear it."

Ro pressed her lips together, drew in a quick breath. "I'm leaving," she said. "And I'm taking Rowan with me."

Instead of backing away, Alma came closer, the expensive flats Rowan had bought her splashing in rainwater. "Why?" she asked.

She stood over Ro, hands at her sides as if waiting for a reason to use them.

"He and I…" Dry mouthed, Ro flicked a nervous middle finger into her throat's hollow. She could feel the badly healed bone click and pop. "… we just can't stay here. I'm sorry."

"Why?" Alma watched her, seemed to be mesmerized by the movement of Ro's finger. She crossed her arms at her waist, dug nails into her elbows. The engagement ring threw daggers of light in Ro's eyes.

Ro stumbled to her feet, crashing into the coffee mug. It cracked open and spilled around her bare feet, burning her toes, running into the rainwater on the stone terrace. She barely felt the pain.

"He can't do this right now. I can't do this."

Ro left Alma on the terrace in the ruins of spilled coffee and tears. The ache of it was too much. Her stomach hurt. Her head pounded. Her body felt too ridiculously out-of-control.

She left Nelson's house and somehow was back at the home Rowan had bought. She closed and locked the front door, intending to fall back into the bed, drying blood stains on the sheets be damned. But the bed had been made. The sheets changed. They had been spot-cleaned and hung on the back line to dry. The gray sheet flapped in the wind, the lone piece of cloth on the line, snapping in mockery at Ro.

Alma had cleaned up after her. Had she even thought about what those stains meant?

In the backyard, Ro clenched her hands in her pockets, breathed in the faint dampness of the morning, the quiet serenity of the house Rowan had designed and built, and carefully nurtured for five years.

Rowan had always valued his privacy. The house's windows were smoke grey glass that kept out the sun and the eyes of strangers, and the backyard had the highest fence of any in the neighborhood. He didn't want to be seen.

But Alma was different. Her house on the hill was full of light. The windows were barred but poured in sunlight from every angle. She kept pillows on the living room floor under the wide three paneled windows where she would often lay in the sun and read. When she started to visit Rowan more often, he wanted to make her comfortable, and so he built a place for her in the backyard. A shed transformed just for her. Tall cathedral style windows were built into the three walls of the small house, even the front door was glass-paneled so Alma could be in the house and never be without light. Shutters pulled down over the windows when she wasn't visiting, but otherwise it was open and just for her.

But she would never visit again.

Breath shuddered in Ro's throat. This, among many things, was what she'd lost in the transformation. She had to accept that, and she had to leave. She looked at the garden and the back yard and Alma's little house one more time. Then turned her back on it all.

In the bedroom, she pulled the most androgynous and comfortable of Rowan's clothes from the drawers and closets, and threw them on the bed next to an open duffel bag. She was stuffing the clothes into the bag when the tap of footsteps jerked her head up. Alma stood in the doorway with the keys to Ro's house dangling in her hand.

"You can't leave," Alma said. Dried tears lined her face, but she looked determined enough to stop a tank in its tracks.

***

The day Rowan met Alma, a tally of hungers had been building inside him. All the things he wanted but thought he could never have. A lover who knew him completely. Children. The perfect flavor and texture of Great Nut ice cream.

He sat at the back of the UWI Mona lecture hall, supposedly waiting on a talk by a visiting Japanese genius, but in actuality was sticking around for newly tenured Nelson to finish teaching his last class of the day so they could ride their motorcycles down to the beach. Rowan didn't feel like waiting in the sun and the lecture hall seemed like as good a place as any. On stage, a thin Asian man, Japanese presumably, stepped up to the podium and began to speak. In Japanese.

Around him, people picked up headphones from their desks and put them on. It was like a scene from one of those movies about the UN. Following the cues, Rowan put on his own set of headphones. Instantly, a warm female voice wrapped around his ears, blocking out every other noise.

The voice wasn't British, it wasn't American. It was something in between that made him cross his legs, then check if anyone else in the room was having the same problem. No one seemed to. The voice was a warm glove, a parody of professionalism, the English words translating the Japanese seamlessly, talking about trade and treaties and opportunities across the sea, when all Rowan wanted to do was slip his hands through the headphones, into the wet cocoon of that voice and stroke it, slide his tongue along its ridges and slippery curves until it grew breathless and all its talk of treaties and trade and foreign opportunities turned to "fuck me" and "harder" and "right there!"

Rowan flushed hot under his shirt, pants pulling tight, throat dry. All because of an anonymous voice through used headphones.

He stayed until the end of the lecture, ignoring Nelson's texts and vibrating phone calls. At the end of the session, the man at the podium raised his gray head and cast bespectacled eyes over the auditorium. The voice in Rowan's ear asked, "any questions?" the same time that a woman came from behind the curtain. Elegant shoes, a pale skirt suit, and a face that was all calm.

She had a medium-sized mouth. Medium skin tone. Eyes a medium width apart. Her natural hair bloomed black and healthy around a face that was, by turns and depending on the arc of the light, arresting or forgettable.

The woman pointed to someone in the audience who had their hand raised the same time she walked down the short set of stairs with a microphone in her hand. She translated the resulting question into Japanese. Or more importantly, she made Rowan lose his breath and lean further across the desk to take a better look, to watch her mouth wrap around the foreign words like she was a sorceress reaching into his most secret thoughts and fantasies and bringing them to soft-fleshed life.

175

He raised his hand. And it was a breathless pleasure to watch her walk, this woman in her sensible shoes and pale suit. She tilted the mic toward his mouth to retrieve the question. She smelled like freshly printed paper, hot and dry, businesslike and tempting to sweaty hands.

"I would like to have dinner with you tonight," he said into the mic. "Would it be possible?"

The woman turned and began to translate the invitation, he assumed, before she stopped, lips parted. The crowd laughed. On stage, the Japanese gentleman looked amused. He said something and the woman's lashes fluttered over her eyes, resting for a moment on her cheeks. She shook her head, but before she could say a word, Rowan spoke again.

"I won't pressure you," he said. "Your voice is every sinful thing a grown man can imagine."

Her lashes fluttered again, but amusement turned up the corners of her mouth. She tapped a button on her mic. "This is very flattering," she said, "but I don't date students."

Her voice caressed him all the way down to his toes, a slow flickering of syllables and intonation of both *come hither* and *stay away* that held him stiff in his seat.

"It's a good thing I'm not a student then." He handed her his card.

She looked at the card but did not take it. She smiled at him once again before touching the mic's control and walking off to find someone with a more appropriate question. Rowan shamelessly watched her for the rest of the presentation and only roused himself when his phone rang again. Nelson saying he was going to find another friend to go riding with if Rowan didn't get his shit together.

He left the auditorium, but not before finding out her name: Alma Reese. The university's new in-house translator.

The next time they met, it was Alma who found Rowan.

Rowan hadn't been able to stop thinking about her. But he let her be. He did tell Nelson about her though, nearly everything he could remember. But there was one thing he couldn't share. And that was the naked way he felt while looking at her, as if she saw into him completely and clearly. Like an MRI or x-ray machine that was simply doing its job. Maybe that was all, she did this to everyone around her, illuminating their pleasures, their faults, their desires, and left them naked and pulsing, vulnerable to her in a way they had never been before.

And that had just been one meeting. One meeting where they barely said anything to each other. But, living the kind of life he did, Rowan knew things that should not be possible sometimes were. He also allowed for the likelihood that it was all one sided. Maybe she didn't feel the same way, and just saw him as another man who wanted to conquer her beauty.

Exactly a week passed. Rowan came back to the university to see Nelson. He and his friend sat on benches in the sun, drinking Ting grapefruit soda and plotting the weekend. Nelson had a faculty meeting so he couldn't leave campus. Rowan just wasn't ready to go home yet. The sun felt decadently warm on his shoulders and back through the thin T-shirt he wore. He was simply enjoying being in his skin.

Nelson was being himself, talking about a young woman in that morning's meeting who he was half-heartedly trying not to sexually harass.

"You have no idea how many times I imagined her bent over that chair." Nelson took a sip from his green soda bottle. "She is so goddamn sexy. Why did they hire her? Was it just to spite me?"

"I'm going to assume they just wanted to fill the position," Rowan said. "They don't want you to fill *her* position, if you know what I mean. I doubt they took your inappropriate behavior into account."

Nelson was gearing up to defend his ridiculousness when a warm presence appeared at Rowan's side.

"Whatever happened to that dinner invitation?"

Rowan didn't have to look up to see who spoke. That voice was unmistakable, in any language. He closed his eyes. It didn't matter that Nelson was sitting right there. His heart stuttered in his chest and his mouth dried. After a quick moment, he opened his eyes and looked.

Alma stood next to him in another sensible suit, perfect for the warm Jamaican afternoon, perfect for her. She loosely held a briefcase in front of her with both hands. She wore the same smile.

Rowan cleared his throat. "I hadn't heard from you," he said.

"And I hadn't heard from *you*, Rowan Anderson."

Rowan didn't hide his pleasure that she'd found him. He held out his hand. "It's good to see you again," he said. "How about dinner tonight?"

"Dinner tonight works just fine for me." Her touch was warm and dry. Still, it started a fluttering in his chest and a tightening low in his belly. Alma gave him her card with her phone number. "Call me with the place and I'll meet you there." It made sense since he could be a serial killer, or telemarketer.

"I'll call you tonight." Rowan pocketed the card.

"Damn! Did you just jizz in your pants?"

Thankfully, Nelson asked the question after Alma had already walked away, the click of her heels fading on the sidewalk like bedroom music.

Rowan didn't have anything to say. The feel of her was still washing over his skin, the way she smelled, the provocation of her voice. He put the soda bottle to his lips just to moisten his throat so he could talk again.

"Jizz is such a disgusting a word," Rowan muttered, wiping at the condensation the bottle dribbled in his lap.

Nelson laughed at him for a long time.

That night, Rowan arrived too early at the agreed upon restaurant. A swarm of butterflies danced in his stomach. Strangely, the nervousness made him feel good, no posturing just a sincere wallowing in his feelings. His

179

desperate masculinity in the past had been a crutch and felt painful. Like he was betraying himself. He and Nelson often talked about what it meant to be a man, particularly in Jamaica; what it meant to be a man who loved women, but who was expected to act as if they didn't even *like* women in order to get them into bed.

So Rowan arrived at the restaurant with his nervous belly, hoping Alma would continue seeing who he was, and he would clearly see her in return.

At the bottom of the stairs leading up to the rooftop restaurant, he stood waiting. It was a Wednesday, not busy, just the light crowd of a lazy weekday evening. Summertime. The sound of conversation rippling down from the restaurant, Gregory Isaacs singing about his only lover.

He didn't see Alma when she parked but, with the sound of high heels on the cement walkway, he turned and caught her walking toward him in her black dress, her hair brushed up and away from her striking face, that small smile saying both nothing and everything.

It was ironic really, that *she* seemed changeable. In the university auditorium, she was tall and imposing with her impressive suit and professional air. But walking underneath the yellow lamps of the restaurant's parking lot with her slow and deliberate steps, she seemed smaller, a woman coming in from the cold of a long day, soft and smiling. But maybe that was just a lie he told himself as quivering want snaked through his belly and up into his chest making warmth in his cheeks and offering a stuttering hello.

"I'm glad you could come," Rowan said.

"Why wouldn't I?" Alma tilted her head, her mouth held in that now familiar half smile. "After all, you were the one who made me chase you."

She came closer, smelling of the night, and of bottled flowers. She smiled wider this time. "You're very beautiful," she said.

Rowan blushed and cursed himself for doing it. "Men are not beautiful," he said although the mirror often told him differently.

"Lucky for me then that *you* are." She tucked her small purse under her arm. "Are you ready to go in?"

In the restaurant, he asked for a table on the open terrace that had fresh air and a view of the city and of the hills. Rowan and Alma sat with napkins over their laps and water glasses at their elbows.

The waiter came and left them with wine, pieces of bread, and melting stars of butter. Polite and efficient, he moved around them as if he sensed they had an urgency to be alone. And maybe they did.

With his powerful attraction to Alma, Rowan expected to feel weakened in her presence. He could not forget those first few moments in the university auditorium, when speech had been impossible and logical thought out of reach. But instead, he only felt…seen.

"So," he asked. "Why did you search for me?"

Alma sipped her wine and licked a bit of its kiss from her lips before speaking. "Because I've never met anyone who wants me as much as you do. There were other factors, of course, but that impressed me."

Rowan felt himself blushing again. "You like weak men."

"Not weak, just honest about what they want without trying to overwhelm me with the man they *think* I want them to be."

"And that's not weak?"

"Not at all. It's sexy. It's interesting. We have a messed up idea of what it means to be a man in this world."

Rowan leaned in, elbows braced against the table, chin resting on clasped hands. "As a woman," he asked, smiling. "What do you think it means to be a man in the world, or in Jamaica?"

"It means you don't have to be a dick just because you have a dick. It's possible to be good and still be a man." She sipped her wine again, then picked up a small dinner roll, buttered it with a piece of a star. "I've met too many men who don't understand that."

"Are you assuming that I'm good?"

Her mouth curved up, wet and red in the candlelight. "And that you are a man?" She put the bread in her mouth and chewed.

Rowan's face grew hot again. That might have been his cue then to assert his manhood and make some comment about his penis or about his stamina in the bedroom or even about his tongue or anything that men typically bragged about to women they wanted to fuck. But that route didn't feel right.

Instead of saying any of those things, Rowan shrugged. "I'll let your assumptions stand," he said with half a mind on his own dualities.

"Interesting." Alma looked surprised, eyebrow ticking up. "Tell me about yourself, Rowan Anderson."

Rowan chuckled. "There's nothing really interesting to tell. I'm a man, remember?"

"Don't be a dick." Apparently, she liked the word. "Can we have a conversation and just be ourselves, without any expectations? That's what I thought I would get with you, although—" She laughed, rolling her eyes. "—that is a kind of expectation, isn't it?" Alma reached for her wine again.

Rowan smiled and did what she asked. He told her about his small hobbies and his small job, his mother dying when he was on the cusp of college, about being in Jamaica since he was born and never wanting to leave.

"You *never* want to leave?"

She seemed taken at that, her remarkable voice rising in surprise.

"Why should I? Everything I need is here."

Her fingertip slowly circled the rim of the wine glass while she watched him like he was a particularly fascinating specimen she'd stumbled across. "I guess that makes sense," she said. "As a straight, financially successful, masculine man who doesn't want to ask any questions of Jamaican society, there's no point to you wanting anything else."

"Why do I get the feeling you just told me off, but in a nice way?"

She tilted her head, pursed her lips. "Because you're paranoid?"

"Wanting to live where I'm from doesn't make me an idiot or a country bumpkin."

"I didn't say any of those things."

But that's what he heard. Living in Jamaica was something Rowan found easy to do. If Ro ever came back, with all her inconvenient femaleness, that ease would change. But he didn't want to think of that then, not with a beautiful woman sitting across the table from him with candlelight flickering over her skin and the taste of wine like a blessing on his tongue.

"What about you," he asked. "Why are you here in Jamaica?"

"For that information," she said, "you're going to have to probe a little deeper."

Rowan licked his lips and savored the invitation for what it was. "In that case, perhaps a bit more lubrication will help my cause." He poured her more wine.

It was only the restaurant's limited hours—they closed at 3 a.m.—that forced them to leave. Between bites of flaky fresh caught fish, they talked about Alma's childhood in the United States, her college days in London, the two years she spent in Japan, and her parents who still lived in America and wanted nothing to do with Jamaica. She was a product of everything she'd experienced, her parents' open-hearted upbringing, her own Virgo determination to succeed, her love of pleasure and travel that had taken her all over the world only to lead her back to Jamaica, a place she had grown to love through books, movies, and music. Before searching out the job at the university, she'd never been to Jamaica before.

"If you didn't hate poverty so much." Rowan gestured for Alma to walk ahead of him, navigating the maze of now empty tables covered in black cloth. "I think you'd be a hippy, touring the world with a backpack full of hemp and incense and two pairs of underwear faded from being washed every other day."

She laughed as they walked side by side down the stairs. "Only two pairs?"

"You strike me as the thrifty type."

"I am, when it's worth it."

Then they were at her car, a white Honda Civic, and the night seemed about to be over. Rowan had work the next morning. He was sure Alma did too. But he didn't want her to go. One of the waiters walked past them and toward the back of the restaurant with a full garbage bag, briefly souring the air.

"I would like to drive you home," Rowan said after the smell passed.

Alma reached into her purse for her keys and held them up. "I already have my car here, remember?"

"Then let me follow you home, make sure you're safe."

During dinner, Rowan had gotten used to her voice and its deliciously arousing timbre. But now, away from everyone else and with the night falling intimately around them like a soft blanket, the effect of her voice was undeniable. Rowan wanted to gather her close and kiss her from her ears to her ankles. That desire must have been all too obvious.

"This is not going where you think it is," Alma said. "Even if I do let you escort me home."

"And you know what I'm thinking?" Rowan asked.

"Yes." She licked her lips, her gaze dropping to his mouth. "Because I'm thinking the same thing."

Fuck.

Arousal slammed hard and fast into Rowan. She wanted him. He released a shudder of breath, could barely bring himself to think. Everything was sensation—the way the clothes sat on his skin, the cool feel of the car's roof under his palms as he crowded her against the driver side door, called by her heat and the way she looked up at him in casual challenge.

"Nothing will happen tonight that you don't want," he said.

"I know."

Alma left the restaurant parking lot with Rowan following closely behind. It was quiet in downtown Kingston, with only a few cars winding through the streets, some only pausing at the red lights to check the flow of traffic before continuing through the intersections. He drove for a while, snaking up into the hills until he arrived at a small house neatly placed on an incline with a gate and a dog barking in the yard.

By the time Rowan pulled in after Alma, the neighbor's
verandah light came on, and a young woman, her head
covered in a floral sleep cap, peered over the fence between
the two properties. "Alma, is that you?" she called out.

Rowan thought he saw the shape of a gun under the
woman's floral robe. Alma reassured the woman with a
laughing greeting.

"Everything is cool, Ms. Hyacinth."

The woman retreated after a moment, and her light
went out.

Then she and Rowan walked onto her verandah flooded
with light, their footsteps tapping across the concrete. Alma
slipped the key in the lock but did not open the door.

"I had a good time tonight," she said. "Thank you."

Rowan stepped closer. "Thank you for coming after me
when I'd given up on the hunt."

"I doubt you really gave up," she murmured, leaning
back into the narrow triangle of darkness that lay across the
doorway. "It may not have been today, but I would've
heard from you again."

The angle of her body was invitation itself. Her back
pressed into the dark corner of the doorway, hips tilted out.
She drew Rowan like salt. A flavor he desperately wanted
on his tongue, to savor and suck until all his taste buds
burst with satisfaction. He didn't resist the steady thrum of
arousal through his body that made him move forward until
Alma pressed even more into that corner, her head tipped
back, lips wet and parted to show the gleam of teeth.

"I want to kiss you," she breathed.

"I want you to kiss me."

Beyond the texture and waxy flavor of her lipstick, her mouth tasted like sweet wine. She was softness and restrained desire in the hidden triangle of her doorway. Rowan savored the small parts of her she allowed him, the pouty curve of her mouth, the soft noises she made, her thighs moving more restlessly the deeper their kisses became. Rowan gasped into her mouth, fingers digging into her hips. He moved desperately against her, circling his own hips, groaning as the thick heaviness in his lap grew, a wanting that threatened to overcome all reason.

He pulled away, taking soft pecking kisses of her lips and moving back into the light, but she followed, moaning softly, her fingers wrapping around the back of his neck and raking up into his hair. She bit down into his lower lip, and he was lost.

"Let's go inside…" He stroked her thigh, tugged up her skirt. Desperation made his movements jerky and graceless.

"No." She slid a thigh between his. "Not on a first date."

Rowan's breathing stuttered with the filthy stroke of her thigh. "Alma…" He pulled back, panting, his spine tight with desire.

She cupped between his legs.

Jesus… "If you keep touching me… If you keep touching me—fuck! I won't last."

Rowan shoved her hand away and reached instead for the buttons of her dress. Alma moaned with approval, her head falling back to thud into the wall. She wasn't wearing a bra. Rowan unbuttoned all the way down to her waist, hissing with appreciation of her high breasts, the dark nipples that tempted his mouth. He stroked Alma's breasts and she trembled, gasping with each brush of his thumbs over her nipples.

"You feel so…You feel..." Her words trailed off into gasping breaths. She seemed more sensitive there than any woman he had ever touched, every stroke provoked a quiver, every tug on her nipples made her circle her hips against his, heated movements that tempted him beyond reason.

"I want your mouth. Please!" Her whispers were broken, wrecked noises.

Rowan gathered her breasts in both hands, stroking the sensitive peaks with each pass, his mouth going lower, kissing her jaw, the slight bitterness of her perfume behind her ear, the shivering line of her throat. By the time his mouth hovered over her breasts, her fingers were gouging into his neck, demanding.

Rowan licked the firm bud of one nipple, tenderly stroked the other.

"Please..." She panted. "Don't tease me."

He gave her what she wanted, a firm suck and release, wet worship of the hard peaks, tongue fluttering and firm. Alma's chest heaved under his mouth, her body a quivering mess held upright between him and the doorframe.

Rowan smelled her. The heat of her arousal, her woman's body eager to be pleased. He dropped to his knees, panting to taste, pushed her skirt up, pulled her panties down.

His mouth watered.

In the dark, he couldn't see but could feel, could touch, could taste. A broken off cry sounded above him, like she slapped a hand across her own mouth. He pushed her thighs wider, baring her pussy to his gaze. Rowan shivered. When was the last time a woman affected him this way? When was the last time it wasn't just about fucking? He wanted to delve inside her, not just into her pussy, but into everything she was. He licked her, hairs scraping his face, wet and musky. He parted the lush bush and dove into the salty wet center of her.

"Oh god oh god oh god oh god…"

Alma shuddered while she fucked Rowan's mouth and groaned into her own hand. But it wasn't enough. Rowan wanted more. He draped her legs over his shoulders, holding her up completely and pressing her thighs wider, pushing his tongue deeper. Alma shuddered and bucked. Cried out. Rowan flicked his tongue and sucked, alternating the suction and strokes until she was writhing into his face and panting his name.

"Your mouth is…just as beautiful as the rest of you…"

He gripped her thighs and hummed. Alma's back snapped away from the doorframe, and she exploded all over his face. He eased her down with delicate strokes of her slick folds, pulling back slowly until her feet were once again on the ground.

"Oh God..." She panted between the words, hands trembling where they grabbed at Rowan's shoulders, nails digging through the thin cotton of his shirt. "That's not why I invited you here. I promise."

"It's all right." Rowan swallowed thickly, willing away the blinding cloud of his arousal. "Next...*fuck*...next time, you can make it up to me." He pressed the heel of a hand into the firm throbbing between his thighs.

Rowan licked the slick from his lips and stood up. Alma's mouth, red and only slightly pink now from her lipstick, was swollen from when she bit into it, coming with Rowan's face between her thighs. He wanted to kiss her, push into the house and fuck in her bed, then make love in her shower. But he had the feeling none of that would happen tonight.

"I'll let you go inside now. It's getting late." And he had an urgent appointment with his hand at home. If he could make it that far.

"See you in a few days?" Alma's breath huffed into the night's quiet.

"Yes," he said. "Soon."

"Tomorrow?"

"Yes!" Rowan backed away, but waited until Alma was safely inside her house before walking carefully down the set of stone steps to the car. Despite the insistent hardness in his slacks and the image of Alma and her spit-slicked nipples that burned in his mind's eye, Rowan kept both hands on the steering wheel the whole way home. But it was hard.

Alma kept Rowan on his toes over the next two years, never allowing him to get too used to anything except the fact that she wanted him. When he knew she loved him, and was certain that he loved her, he proposed. Then everything went to shit.

***

In the bedroom Rowan had shared with Alma too many times to count, Alma confronted Ro. "You can't leave."

Ro wished Alma's voice didn't have such a strong effect on her. Over time it had become less sex and more connection, less seduction and more completion, Alma's voice that always reminded her of home. The breath hissed between Ro's teeth.

Alma was...awake. Rowan had always liked that in the morning, Alma was softer, a silken woman lying in sheets where she had been properly made love in, spread out for herself and for him, delicate. But as the day wore on, she drew her armor more tightly around her, becoming the professional, the woman who lived in a dangerous city, a woman not to be fucked with. That was the Alma who stood in front of Ro now.

"*You* should leave," Ro said. "There's nothing for you here."

"Bullshit."

Yes, Alma of the morning was definitely gone.

Alma crossed her arms tight over her chest, claiming the doorway as if to stop Ro from leaving. "Rowan and I worked to create a successful and happy relationship over the last two years. We mean a lot to each other. I deserve more than his unexplained disappearance."

"He's just gone, dammit! Accept that."

Frustration broke inside Ro. She was losing absolutely everything. Rowan was gone for good; she could feel it now as surely as she could feel the menstrual ache of her womb. And that meant Alma was gone too.

"I'll never accept it. Not from anyone but him." Alma tightened her grip on her elbows. Her jaw shifted with the clench of her teeth.

She looked determined, the expression on her face like she was trying to solve a problem that was nearly unsolvable, something she knew she could handle and break apart and put together again. But this thing was unfixable. Rowan was gone and would never come back.

"I can't lose him," Alma said, her voice breaking.

The pain on her face was almost too much for Ro to take. Alma was tough. Not all the time, but in front of strangers she held herself in a way that was like a fortress, impenetrable and strong. From what Alma knew, Ro *was* a stranger. But her chin wobbled.

Please don't cry, Ro silently begged.

But a sob cracked open Alma's throat. It wailed into the room, a sound of desolation and despair that nearly brought Ro to her knees. She steadied herself against the bed.

"I can't bring him back—" The words tumbled out of Ro. "—because he and I are the same. I *am* Rowan."

Alma blinked at her, eyes wide and wet with sadness. But anger tightened her mouth. "If you don't want to tell me the truth, then don't. Just don't fucking lie to me like a *stranger.*" Then she bit her lip, her brows wrinkling as she seemed to think about what she just said. "Please, tell me where he is."

"Why would I lie to you about something like that? Fuck! If it was up to me, I'd still have his body. I'd still have you."

Alma's lashes fluttered, and she looked away, her mouth falling open, her hand pressed to her chest. "This is really crazy," she said softly, looking dazed. "This is—" then she cut herself off, biting her lip. She looked at Ro's finger, the finger that had been unconsciously flicking at her throat's hollow. Ro dropped her hand. "I can't—" Alma turned and ran out of the room.

This was what she wanted, right? Right?

But Ro didn't realize she was moving until she bumped her shoulder into the doorway of the bedroom, rushing after Alma who was running toward the front door and away.

This is what you want. Let her go. Let her find happiness with someone who can be a man for her.

The front door pushed open under Alma's frantic hands, slammed back against the wall, and rebounded into Ro's face. She shoved it open and the day was there, stretched out before her. Bright sun, bright flowers, the untamed blue of the sky, but might as well have been darkness for all Ro was feeling. She grabbed Alma's arm and yanked her to a standstill.

Alma spun to face her, her teeth flashing white with anger. "What do you want from me now?"

"I want—"

"Alma! Is that you?" Felice, Rowan's neighbor, stood a few feet from the front gate staring up at them, hands on her hips. "What kind of homosexual business are you dealing with up there on Rowan's property?"

"Mind your business, woman!" Alma never liked Felice. Ever since Alma began to visit Rowan, Felice regularly came by the house hinting at a shameful and unforgivable past of Alma's that Rowan had no idea about.

Ro's grip on Alma's arm loosened. "Come on baby, you know she's only jealous Rowan never paid any attention to her daughter." Ro bit into her tongue. She just talked to Alma like she was still Rowan, still with the right to call her 'baby.'

"How did you know –?" Alma looked up at Ro, that familiar wrinkle of confusion floating away to become something else. "Rowan..."

But she wasn't that anymore. "My name is Ro," she said. "Will you come with me so we can talk?"

Ro didn't know what she wanted to say, but she had to say something. Watching Alma nearly run away made her realize that letting Alma leave wasn't something she could easily do. Not without an explanation.

"Come," she said again.

Some of the tension leaked from Ro when Alma allowed herself to be led into the backyard and to the glass and wooden sanctuary Rowan had built for her. The small, one room structure was just as Alma left it the last time she visited. A tumble of pillows strewn on the rug-covered floor, dozens of unlit candles along all four walls, a pair of clean tea-cups and an unfinished Scrabble game on the wooden coffee table. Everything else was just open space, glass allowing in the day's light.

Ro sat on one of the pillows and invited Alma to join her. Still with her eyes wide, Alma sat down. She crossed her legs like a genie, clasped her hands in her lap.

"I don't understand," she said after taking a breath. "You look like—no, you *are* him." She waved her hand to indicate Ro's body, looking pointedly at her once broken finger.

The explanation, Ro thought. *This was the time.*

"I'm…my mother called us gendermorphs," she began quietly. "The gender of our bodies is not fixed but fluid. The transformations are triggered by hormonal or even extreme emotional changes." Ro remembered her mother, how consistently female she'd been except for that spring she became Ro's father, storm-faced after her rape by a co-worker. A co-worker who'd ended up dead a week later. "I've never known any others except me and my mother." Her finger flicked. "But I assume they're out there." She shrugged. "Mama never explained much about who we are or where we came from, and I've been too scared to search on my own."

Her mother hadn't told Ro much more except to say she would change for most of her life, then one day it would just stop at the gender she was born with.

It was hard to explain to Alma about growing up with her mother who was always protective of their lives, and who never let anyone else get close to them. But Ro tried her best.

She told Alma about being born a girl, then changing after three weeks; the years of being Rowan; waking up at thirteen to blood on her thighs, her mother comforting her, taking care of her girl's body until, barely a month later, Rowan came back. And stayed for nineteen years.

Silence. The shift of Alma's face from confusion to shock to betrayal. More silence.

"Why didn't you tell me?" Alma stared at Ro.

"How could I tell anyone that? You didn't believe me at first. Even now I'm not sure that you do believe. Plus…" Ro looked down at her hands, long and slender, just like Rowan's. "It was private."

Alma winced at the last word.

Shit.

"I didn't mean…" Ro reached toward Alma, but Alma pulled away.

She drew one of the pillows into her lap, squeezing it like it would stop her from throttling Ro. "You've had your dick in every orifice of my body, my fingers and tongue have been in every one of yours, we're about to promise to spend our lives together. And now you're saying something between us is *private?*"

Fuck. Ro tried to backpedal without quite telling Alma the truth. Although the truth was as easy to see as the pair of breasts outlined through her shirt. "It's not like I'm hiding money from you," Ro said desperately.

"I will turn and walk away if you don't stop acting like the dick you no longer have."

At the mention of that now non-existent part of her anatomy, Ro felt like the air had been jabbed out of her stomach. It hurt. And it pulled the truth out of her.

"I was afraid that if you knew, you'd leave me."

The truth popped between them like an overgrown pustule. But now that it was out there, Ro couldn't quite face it. Abruptly, she turned away from Alma to stare outside as if it held the balm to her misery.

But the day's beauty was painful to see. The garden was beautiful and everything Rowan had planted burst with colorful life. Rowan had never been one for emotional honesty. He desired Alma. He could tell her and did tell her as often as he felt it. But he never talked about his deep and sometimes overwhelming love for her. He never discussed his insecurities, his stubborn clinging to what defined him as a man. Even after saying to himself that he was no longer the one who had to act a certain way to proclaim his manhood.

"I want you," he'd said a thousand times.

"I love you," he'd never said, and would never get the chance to say.

At Ro's back, Alma shifted. Her hand drifted to Ro's hip and slid under her T-shirt already warming in the sun. "If you think I'd leave you because of something like this, then maybe you don't know me as well as I thought." Alma said the words almost thoughtfully. "But I think that's my fault."

Her touch on Ro's hip was even warmer than the sun, fingers moving in soothing circles. "I think it's my turn to tell you a story," she said. After a long hesitation, she began to speak again.

"From the time I was in middle school in the States, maybe even before, I knew I was bisexual."

What?

Ro turned to stare at Alma. Her Alma, the woman Rowan had known for two years and loved for almost that long, looked back at Ro with an eyebrow raised, her lips pursed.

"But, I was bisexual only in theory. I loved girls. I preferred them over any of the boys or men I met."

Alma lived her life in America then in England then in Japan, falling in love and having sex with women, not finding a single man she could invite into her life or even into her body. And then she met Rowan Anderson. "When I talked to Rowan in that lecture hall, I felt something for a man I *never* had before. He was so damn beautiful, and the way he wanted me literally made my knees weak."

Ro flashed back to their second meeting, the determined way Alma pursued Rowan, the ease of that first passion-filled night pressed into her doorway. Was that how she'd been with women?

Ro opened her mouth to ask Alma if she'd stay, but something entirely different came out of her mouth instead. "You're bisexual?"

Alma pulled slightly away. "Yes. Do you have a problem with that?"

Ro shook her head, dazed. Relieved. "Why didn't you ever tell Rowan?" But just as she asked the question, Ro realized what Alma's answer would be.

"It was *private*." Her eyebrow jerked up on the last word, obviously not serious, but still irritated by Ro's earlier comment.

Okay, Ro deserved that. There were some things she should never do with Alma. And shielding something from her in the name of privacy was definitely one of them.

"Have we been different people for each other all this time?" she asked.

Alma's fingers tightened on Ro's hip. "Not different, aslant." She bit her lip in uncertainty, something Ro hadn't seen in a long time, not since the very first days of their relationship. "I won't say that your transformation isn't a surprise," Alma said. "But it's also kind of like winning the lottery." A tentative smile curved her mouth. "A two for one."

Ro felt a spark of surprise she couldn't hide.

"My mother, she embraces magic in a way that I never could," Alma continued. "When I called her earlier today, before I came back over here, I told her everything."

"What?" She knew before Ro told her?

"When I saw your broken finger and the way you touched your throat like you always do, I suspected," Alma said while Ro stared open-mouthed at her, rocked by another surprise. "It seemed so crazy, but how else to explain period blood on the sheets you and I slept in when it didn't come from me?" Alma nibbled on her fingertip, looked slyly through her lashes at Ro. "Anyway, my mother believed it right away. And do you know what she said to me? She said I'd found one of the rarest things, true love with someone I actually like and with someone who likes me as a person. And that I should do whatever I need to keep you in my life. Ro or Rowan or in between."

Alma dropped her hand back in her lap, drew a deep breath. "I love you, Ro. This is me embracing magic."

Oh my God.

Ro curled her fingers into her palms until it hurt.

Is this really happening?

The light all around them felt like it was piercing Ro's skin. It slid into her, sharp and bright and burning in a way she sometimes imagined the change from Ro to Rowan, or vice versa, would feel. But this was the sensation of Alma's acceptance, her true and naked love. The tears pricked her, salt and sweet, and rolled down her face.

"I've been an ass," she said with the taste of tears on her lips.

"Yes, you have." Alma slipped her hand into Ro's. "But I love you anyway."

Ro lay down and put her head in Alma's lap as she'd always done, and breathed deeply with gratitude. It felt the same, Alma's touch in her hair and down her neck. The usual transcendental bliss. She was a fool to have doubted.

***

The morning after Ro married Alma, she woke up content, her body sore but still hers, still sated from last night's love. The change from Rowan to Ro was over a year in the past and she had grown into her new life, grown into this incarnation of her love for Alma.

She stretched out in the bed. A salt breeze whispered over her naked body from the open windows on both sides of the bedroom. After only a year of this, it should have felt strange to stretch out with the wind brushing the delicate folds between her legs, licking at the curves of her breasts. But, it only felt...normal. A job secured in Florida, the Jamaican house rented, their honeymoon begun in Key West.

Things had not fallen into the pit like Ro had imagined the year before. In fact, she—

"Well, this is something I could get used to seeing for the rest of my life."

Ro turned, mouth quirked, to see her wife next to her. Her hair still neatly braided from the wedding, the sheets low on her hips, her smile full and sleepy.

"That's good," Ro said, "because you're not getting rid of me any time soon."

A smile drifted over Alma's face like the sun. "After all we've been through, it's good to hear you say that."

"I know." Even now, Ro felt foolish about what she'd decided the year before without telling Alma what they were facing. By agreeing to get married, they already decided to live their lives together, and then the next day Ro was taking that promise back. But that was in the past.

Ro touched Alma's face, breathed in the sleep scent of her and sighed. "You are the woman of my life."

"And you are the love of mine."

They said the words that had become familiar to them over the past year, part of their wedding vows, the expression of their unending bond to each other no matter what Ro became, no matter the brightness of the stars in the skies. Breath huffed against Ro's mouth and she wrinkled her nose, smiling. "Your breath is poison, baby," she said although hers probably smelled the same.

"Oh, really? Like yours is so sweet." Alma shoved at Ro while Ro backed away, laughing and holding up her hands. But when Alma's mouth landed on hers, she parted her lips eagerly accepting the wet pressure of her tongue, the sweetness that lay in her mouth, hidden then unearthed beneath that taste of sleep and waking. Her body quickened easily, a familiar heat, and wetness between her legs, her nipples firming in readiness for Alma's mouth.

They slid together in the bed, shoving the sheets away.

Yes, it had been a year, but *this* still felt new, still felt beautiful, the aroused slick of her thighs and her wetness that eagerly swallowed Alma's fingers, even the greedy, nipping kisses Alma preferred to give that felt sharper in this new skin, the sure grasp of her fingers around Ro's hips like an anchor in this new life.

"I love you," Ro gasped into Alma's mouth as her hips jerked and she spilled over in release. "I love you!"

Alma was already rising up from Ro's breasts, breathless and smiling. "Show me, baby." She moved up in the bed to spread the wet perfection of her pussy over Ro's lips. "Show me how much you love me."

The soft slick of her touched Ro's mouth, settled on her lips and Ro groaned. She slid her questing tongue into the heart of her new wife as if she meant to stay there, somehow, for a lifetime.

THE END

Thank you for reading!

About the Author

Jamaican-born Fiona Zedde currently lives and writes in Atlanta, Georgia. She is the author of several novellas and novels of lesbian love and desire, including the Lambda Literary Award finalists Bliss and Every Dark Desire. Her novel, Dangerous Pleasures, was winner of the About.com Readers' Choice Award for Best Lesbian Novel or Memoir of 2012. Her latest novel, Desire at Dawn, featuring the vampire clan from Every Dark Desire, is available now.

Find out more at www.FionaZedde.com

Made in the USA
Columbia, SC
13 July 2017